To Claim His Highland Bride

TO CLAIM HIS HIGHLAND BRIDE

A GUARDIANS OF THE ISLES ROMANCE

GERRI RUSSELL

TULE

Where your pleasure is, there is your treasure: where your treasure, there your heart; where your heart, there your happiness.

—*Saint Augustine*

DEDICATION

To April Rickard. You are a sister of my heart and the wind beneath my wings.

PROLOGUE

Loch Dunvegan, Isle of Skye, Scotland
September 15th, 1742

T HE MORNING BREEZE tugged at Rowena MacLeod's hair as she stood alongside her one true love, Marcus, at the shore of Loch Dunvegan. Her brother, Alastair, and his wife, Gwendolyn, stood behind them at a distance, giving her and Marcus privacy as they said goodbye.

Rowena's gaze strayed to Marcus's ship in the distance. *The Cliodna* would take him away from her for the next year. "Must you go?" she asked with sudden despair. "I am content to live at Dunvegan Castle for the rest of our lives at the mercy of my brother if that's what we must do in order to be together." They could hide from their troubles with the MacDonald clan within the safety of her brother's mighty fortress. They could carve out a niche of fairy-tale happiness away from all those who did not approve of a MacDonald marrying a MacLeod.

Marcus looked at her in surprise. "I'll not be beholden to your clan for my livelihood—no matter how much I love you, Rowena. Every last bit of wealth I had I used to purchase *The Cliodna*. That ship is the only way forward for us both. Since I have no home, no clan, no funds to offer you, I have no choice but to leave. I must find my own way forward using the only thing that is truly mine—my ship."

Rowena traced her fingertips over the muscles of Marcus's chest and felt the beat of his heart beneath. After all that they'd been through together already, she had hope that a small part of his heart longed to stay beside her as much as she longed for him. "I could come with you."

He took her in his arms. "The sea is an unforgiving mistress at times. I'll not put your life in danger."

"I'm not afraid of danger." She tensed in his arms. Why did every person in her life think her incapable of enduring misfortune? They all wanted to keep her safe behind the walls of Dunvegan, as if she wasn't strong or clever enough to protect herself. Hadn't she recently proven that she was? Twice? Yet no one seemed to remember the moments of danger she'd come through unscathed. To them, she was a butterfly, too fragile and delicate for anything other than observation. Butterflies did not go to war, or out to sea, or even beyond the gates of Dunvegan without an escort. "I'm not fragile, Marcus. I can take whatever the sea has in store for me."

"Rowena . . ." His voice became softer, more desperate. "I cannot take you with me, and I can only leave you if I know you are safe and protected with your brothers at Dunvegan. You know better than anyone what I must do to secure a better life for us both."

Rowena clenched her jaw, wanting to argue, but knowing it would get her nowhere. Not when Marcus's gaze held the ferocity it did now. Instead, she lifted her hands to his cheeks. "I wish Alastair had agreed to let us marry."

Marcus lowered his mouth to hers, kissing her with all the tenderness and passion mirrored in her own heart. But as he lifted his lips, a numb, empty feeling settled inside her. This was a goodbye kiss. No amount of arguing or kissing would change his mind. He was leaving her to secure a future for them.

The sea is an unforgiving mistress. Marcus's words came back to her. The moment he left the shores of Dunvegan their future would be unknown. Marcus's life would be in constant danger, not only from the sea, but from the dangerous activities of a privateer. She might never see him again.

An impending sense of loss swamped her as Rowena released her hold on Marcus to wrap her shaking limbs about herself.

"I will come back to you as soon as I am able."

Rowena blinked to keep the tears back as the salt-laden breeze stirred her hair. She pulled her tartan shawl closer about her shoulders as the numbness she'd felt moments ago moved deeper inside her.

"I can delay my parting no longer," Marcus said with a catch in his voice.

An instant before he turned towards the waiting boat

that would take him out to his ship, Rowena saw Marcus's face in sharp detail: his green eyes filled with sorrow, a strong jawline, his wide sensual mouth, the truant lock of dark brown hair that fluttered against his brow.

"I will wait for your return every night." She pressed her lips together to keep herself from saying anything more. She would not plead with him to stay. He was convinced this was the only way forward for the two of them. Even though she tried to look at the water instead, her gaze moved back to Marcus, and the ache in her chest grew until it threatened to smother her.

With one last kiss, Marcus turned and headed for the boat. He shoved the boat away from the shore and leapt inside. Instead of watching him leave, she focused on the water of the loch. The waves rose gently and curled over a wash of foam, glittering in the early morning light as they slid against the beach before slipping back again. When she could avoid looking at Marcus no longer, her gaze lifted to see him standing in the boat with his fists at his sides, his face expressionless as the boat took him farther from her.

Gwendolyn and Alastair came to stand beside her. "I'll take good care of her," Alastair called to Marcus.

Marcus nodded, keeping his gaze fixed on Rowena as the oarsmen rowed the boat into the deeper waters where *The Cliodna*, Marcus's brigantine, waited.

Rowena's hair whipped in the wind as she watched his transfer boat disappear into the shadow of *The Cliodna*.

Within minutes, sheets of the wide, white canvas were unfurled on her two tall masts, straining and swelling eagerly in the stiff winds. Marcus and his crew would be out into the open sea before the sun reached its zenith.

I will wait for you. Rowena let her tears fall even as they were snatched away by the wind. The look in Marcus's eyes moments ago reflected his love for her, but a year changed people. Would he still feel the same when he returned to the shores of Dunvegan? If he returned at all? Would she? They had only the promise of a betrothal between them, but nothing beyond that.

Would that whispered agreement be enough to bind them together during his absence? Only time would tell . . .

CHAPTER ONE

North Sea, Isle of Skye, Scotland
September 30th, 1742

Marcus MacDonald turned his face into the wind and gazed at the point where the North Sea met the sky. Never had he imagined that being a MacDonald fighting for the MacLeods would secure his letters of marque so quickly. He and the crew of *The Cliodna* were now privateers and were authorised by the government to attack enemy ships for their own gain as they sailed off to make their fortunes.

They were heading north-east to the open waters of the Atlantic where they would be tested, Marcus was certain, not just by an unforgiving ocean, but also by the ships they would encounter. Marcus was new to the profession of seafarer and pirate, though as a MacDonald he'd seen his share of combat. His crew was in good hands with him as their captain, and with his first mate, Eckland MacFarlane, who'd been born to the sea. Between the two of them the souls aboard *The Cliodna* would be successful in their endeavours. They had to be. Marcus's very existence and that of his soon-to-be bride depended on his success.

Marcus shifted his gaze to the sails billowing in the wind. They would reach the Atlantic in no time if the winds held. Then their adventure would truly begin. The scent of the sea surrounded him as his gaze shifted yet again to a seabird following in their wake. Marcus would take that as a favourable sign since their ship was named for the otherworld goddess of the sea who took the form of a seabird during the day.

A smile pulled up the corners of his lips when a shout came from the crow's nest above. "Shipwreck ahead to the port side."

"Lower the sails. Maintain our distance to keep us away from unseen dangers," Marcus called to his men as he grabbed his spyglass and moved to the port railing. As the crew gathered the sails and tied the ropes, Marcus peered at the flotsam in the water, identifying parts of a ship but no survivors. Then he spotted a larger portion of the ship's hull and a sodden lump farther from the rest of the wreckage. To his first mate, who had taken the tiller, he shouted, "I see a possible survivor two points forward of port beam. Proceed slow and steady."

When the ship was within range, a rescue boat was lowered. Marcus watched as four of his crew rowed towards the object in the water. They pulled a body into their boat and rowed back to *The Cliodna*. It wasn't long before they had the man stretched out on the deck. Marcus knelt beside him and placed his cheek close to the man's mouth. A soft whisper of breath came from the survivor's mouth. "He's still alive. Bring me several blankets."

As the blankets were placed about the man, Marcus moved the wet strands of his long white and grey hair away from his cheeks to reveal a weathered face. His skin was leathery and pale. The survivor was perhaps seventy, but it was difficult to say as a result of how long the man had been floating in the water and subjected to a chilly autumn wind.

"'Tis a miracle he's alive," Marcus said. "Take him to my cabin and place him on a cot. Bring a bucket of hot rocks to warm him." The crew dispersed to do as Marcus asked while he followed those who took the man to his quarters.

When the survivor of the shipwreck was settled and the crew had departed, Marcus moved a chair closer to the man's cot. They had no one aboard with any kind of medical training except Marcus's own basic survival skills. He hoped that would be enough to help the man before him.

Marcus pulled the covers up higher to better warm the man as heat from the hot rocks warmed the captain's quarters. Several minutes later, Marcus had to remove his surcoat. As the temperature in the chamber increased, the man on the cot started trashing about, though he did not wake.

A knock sounded at the door. "Enter," Marcus bid the unseen crewman.

Eck MacFarlane entered and quickly shut the door behind him to maintain the heat. "How is he doing?"

"Not well," Marcus said. The man on the cot looked pale and weak, though the thrashing of his head back and forth indicated an inner strength. Perhaps that would be enough to see him through this ordeal.

"Will he live?" Eck asked.

Marcus shrugged. "It's really up to him now that he is out of the water and warmed. I got him to take a few sips of broth."

Eck leaned against the cabin wall. "What do you suppose he was doing near Cape Wrath? Everyone who lives near here knows how dangerous that section of water is to navigate. 'Tis not called Cape Wrath for no reason."

"Trea . . . sure," a gravelly voice said.

Both men turned towards the cot. The older man's eyes flickered open. His eyes darted about the cabin before coming to rest on first Marcus and then Eck. "Where . . . am I?"

"You're safely aboard *The Cliodna*," Marcus assured him. "Your ship went down. We found you in the water."

The man swallowed roughly. "Anyone . . . else?"

Marcus pressed his lips together as he shook his head.

"The entire crew? Seven-and-eighty men." The man closed his eyes and sank back against the cot. A mournful sound escaped him.

"We'll give you some time to yourself," Marcus said as he stood and moved towards the door with Eck.

"Nay," the man said. "Must tell you. Before I die."

Marcus and Eck shared a glance then returned to their previous positions. Marcus leaned closer to the cot. "Save your energy. You need to rest."

The man shook his head sadly. "So cold. I can . . . feel death creeping . . . over me." He struggled to sit up, but was too weak.

Marcus reached for the pillow from his own bed and placed it behind the man's head, raising him slightly. "What is your name?" Perhaps his identity would give them a clue as to why he was sailing dangerous waters.

"Jacob Thorne."

Marcus straightened. He'd heard that name over the years associated with some of the most fantastical treasure-hunting stories shared amongst the clans. It was only a couple of years ago that a tale had spread of Jacob Thorne finding the legendary Spanish galleon, *El Grande*, that sank in sixteen hundred and eighty-three. Only four of the four hundred and ninety-six men survived, but not one of them could tell where the ship sank after encountering a hurricane. The ship was said to be carrying silver bullion, spices, gold, pearls, and emeralds.

"Is it true that you found the *El Grande*?" Marcus asked as he carefully studied the man's face. Looking for any signs of deception.

"I did." The hint of a smile pulled up Jacob's lips. "And I brought its treasure back to Scotland."

The pride momentarily shining in Jacob's eyes validated

the claim. Marcus's stomach clenched. 'Twas exactly the type of treasure he himself needed to discover in order to establish a life for himself and Rowena. "If you found such a treasure then why were you out on the sea looking for more?"

"Some men hunt treasure for the money. Others for adventure. I discovered . . . I fall into the latter after my first discovery . . . nearly forty years ago."

Eck straightened. "What did you do with all that bounty? Would there be anywhere safe to store such a treasure?"

Jacob swallowed hard and closed his eyes for a moment before proceeding. "I put fourteen chests filled with treasure in a place . . . no one would think to search . . . the Cave of Gold. Terrifying legends of the place . . . would protect my wealth, but not death." He turned his head towards Marcus. "Recently, I was searching for two Spanish galleons that were said to be laden with gold off the shores of Sandwood Bay. They are there—I know it. My men and I found . . . a few Spanish coins. There are more. Before we could retrieve them, the wind changed . . . It blew our vessel onto the rocks. *The Mandara* broke in two. We had no chance . . . to lower the boats."

"What day was that?" Eck asked, his voice soft.

Jacob's brow furrowed, remembering. "September twenty-fifth."

"Five days ago." A wave of sympathy came over Marcus. It truly was a miracle the man was still alive after being exposed to the elements for so long.

"You saved me . . . so I will tell you. Continue my legacy. Promise to do something good . . . with the treasure." Jacob reached out and curled his cold fingers around Marcus's hand.

Marcus's chest tightened, making it difficult to breathe. "I promise," he said, though he had no idea how he would fulfil what the old man asked.

The man's eyes drilled into Marcus's. "I believe . . . you." His voice was a mere breath of sound.

Marcus released Jacob's hand. "Rest for now. We will talk later."

Jacob shook his head. "I am dying . . . there's no time. Deep in the Cave of Gold . . . I've hidden the fourteen chests. They're yours . . . for trying to help me." His chest rattled with every breath. "The two galleons . . . you'll find them at the bearings I've scratched into the flesh of my arm." He raised his left arm briefly before collapsing onto the cot once more.

Eck frowned down at the dying man. "Why would you hide your gold in a place called 'The Cave of Gold?' Isn't that an invitation for thievery?"

"Too haunted." Jacob's lips tugged up as his face turned even more ashen in colour. "Too dangerous. Perfect hide."

"It is a rather ingenious place," Marcus agreed. "It is said the Cave of Gold is very deep. Some say it extends as far as Fairyland; others say it extends to Hell. It is also rumoured that a ferocious green dog guards the entrance, hiding in the shadows and ready to kill anyone who attempts to enter."

"Saw . . . no dog," Jacob said, the rattling in his chest growing louder.

Marcus offered the man a sympathetic smile. "And if what you say is true, then you are also the first person to come out of the cave alive."

With difficulty, Jacob brought his right hand up over his heart. "Swear . . . what I say is true." His words were slow and pained, then his face went slack and his hand sank down beside him. "Only wish . . . more time to enjoy . . . my efforts."

Marcus reached for the old man's hand. His fingers were icy cold. As Marcus watched the last vestige of colour drain from the man's face, a cascade of emotions came over him. Angst twisted Marcus's gut at the knowledge that Jacob had been saved only to die. And yet a flutter of hope filled his stomach at the thought that what Marcus and his crew sought might be obtained so quickly.

"You do us a great honour, sharing your life's efforts with me and my men. We will find some way to do good with your treasure and to keep the memory of your life alive." That was if they found any treasure, for Marcus was still not entirely convinced what the old man said was true, but Jacob did not need to witness this doubt when his time on this earth was coming to an end.

Jacob's chest rose, then fell slowly, as a deep rattling sound followed.

Marcus swallowed against the thickness in his throat. "Rest in peace, friend."

Jacob squeezed Marcus's fingers lightly as his eyes closed. "Friend . . ." He went still.

Marcus's breath arrested. His chest tightened as Jacob's chest settled.

Several long moments passed as Marcus watched the old man as though waiting for him to take yet another breath. When he did not, Marcus looked to Eck. "He's gone."

Eck nodded. "Do you believe what he said about the Spanish galleons and the Cave of Gold?"

Marcus shrugged as his gaze dropped to the hand he still held. He released Jacob's hand then with both hands forced up the sleeve of his shirt. There, cut into the man's own flesh, were the numbers 58.5396 degrees north by minus 5.0623 degrees east. "He believed in the treasure enough to mar his own flesh with the location."

Eck looked at Marcus inquiringly. "We're close to those coordinates. Is it worth us taking a look?"

The air in the cabin was suddenly charged with possibility. "This man and his crew gave their lives for their belief that the Spanish galleons were there. I'd say we owe them a measure of our time as long as we can keep our own ship safely away from the rocks."

"The men and I can do that." Eck straightened as though awaiting orders.

Marcus rose to his feet. "Send two men here to prepare

Jacob for burial. We will leave him with the rest of his crew in their watery grave." He moved to his desk where he picked up a piece of parchment and his quill, and quickly wrote the coordinates before handing them to Eck. "The rest of the crew should prepare the ship and themselves for the treasure hunt ahead."

Eck's face lit up with his smile. "I imagined our journey to be one of boarding enemy ships, fighting, and looting for our treasures. Never did I imagine diving into the depths of the sea to retrieve them where nature would be our greatest threat."

"Nature is still a force to be reckoned with. None of this will be easy."

Eck reached for the door. "Life often requires a struggle. The men and I are prepared for whatever lies ahead."

Marcus nodded, feeling as much excitement as trepidation. Recovering whatever remained in the wreck of the Spanish galleons would be as dangerous as anything he'd ever done in his life. But if he wanted to create a life for himself and Rowena, independent of her family, he would have to take that risk.

CHAPTER TWO

Dunvegan Castle, Isle of Skye, Scotland
March 14th, 1743

"YOU SHOULD NOT be out here alone at night."
Rowena MacLeod turned to see her oldest brother, Alastair, coming towards the rock on which she sat along the shore of Loch Dunvegan. "You worry too much."

Alastair's brows furrowed in annoyance. "It is my duty to worry about my sister, especially when she is being reckless."

Rowena scowled as Alastair took a seat on the large rock beside her. "There is nothing reckless about sitting along our own castle's shoreline, watching the *Na Fir-Chlis*." The odd green and purple hues of the night sky danced above them. The Northern Lights, the lowlanders called the enchanted night sky. But the MacLeods held tight to Gaelic lore that was the source of many myths and legends, including their own Fairy Flag.

"If you were escorted by one of your brothers, and if that were all you were doing out here alone, I might agree."

Rowena turned away from Alastair to stare into the distant waters of the loch and not the night sky. He knew why she was truly out here. "I watch for Marcus every night. Why should tonight be any different?"

"Aye, but usually you watch for him from the towers of Dunvegan. A much safer location for you." At her frown, he softened his tone. "It has been several months since the MacDonalds or the English have attacked, but that does not mean we should let down our guard."

"It has been six months since Marcus left." Rowena could not hide the anguish in her voice. "Shouldn't he have found his fortune by now?"

"Often it takes years," Alastair said, scooting a little closer. "It took Tormod, Orrick, and me five years to find ourselves and make our own fortunes."

"Five years!" Rowena's eyes rounded as she turned back to her brother. "Nay. It must not take so long. I will not be an old maid when I do finally marry."

"Then perhaps you should look for another bridegroom," Alastair suggested as he placed a gentle hand over hers.

"How can you say such a thing? You know what it is like to love someone, then to lose them. Could you honestly say your life would have been better had you married someone other than Gwendolyn?"

He shook his head. "Nay. Gwendolyn is the only woman I have ever, or will ever, love."

"I feel that way about Marcus despite the fact he is a MacDonald, despite the fact he left me to find his fortune, despite the fact I may never see him again." Her voice drifted off as tears sprang to her eyes.

"Oh, Sister. It pains me to see you like this. Come inside. I'm sure we could talk Mrs Honey into making you a delectable treat that would take your mind off things for a time."

Rowena lifted her chin and forced herself into a calmer state. "I do not want to be mollified, and I refuse to give up on Marcus coming for me sooner rather than later."

Alastair opened his mouth to respond when the sound of rocks shifting beneath someone's feet caught their attention. They turned to see Tormod, yet another one of her meddling brothers, making his way towards them. His hand was on the sword at his side as he searched the darkness as though expecting the enemy to descend upon them at any moment. "We have a very large and very well-protected castle that can keep everyone safe. Yet you insist on staring at the night sky outside of its walls. Why, Sister?"

Rowena released a frustrated breath. Could she have no peace from her family? "I was hoping to find a moment to myself to think."

Tormod stopped before her and relaxed the hand on his weapon. "There are many places where you can be alone inside the castle. Wasn't that one of the reasons you liked to go to the tower rooftop? You can still see the night sky and the waters beyond Loch Dunvegan there."

He had barely finished his words when a cold chill that

had nothing to do with the night came over them. A swirling grey mist swept across the shoreline then coalesced into the shape of a woman, her image growing more solid with each heartbeat until their ghostly mother stood beside them. All the castle residents were used to their mother's frequent appearances and were grateful she was still a part of their lives even though she'd been dead for many years.

I sensed danger. Is everything as it should be out here?

The words resonated in Rowena's head as their mother spoke to them in the only way she could.

Did you both sense danger as well? The Grey Lady's worried gaze shifted between her sons before landing on Rowena, then narrowing. *Why must you leave the castle? It's not safe for you to be alone out here at night.*

Rowena jumped down from her perch on the rock and turned, setting her hands on her hips and glaring with frustration at her family. "Why must all of you treat me as if I am a bird in a cage? As if I'm some fragile thing that needs protection all the time?"

"Because you do not listen," Tormod replied with a stern expression. "You are hot-headed and take far too many risks when it comes to your safety."

She looked to Alastair, hoping he would defend her, but he simply shrugged and said nothing.

"I am not fragile, or have you forgotten when I fought in battle alongside your own wives? I held my own then, as I could do out here should someone creep out of the shadows."

"Fiona was wearing magical armour created by the fairies when she fought beside you in those battles," Alastair reminded her. "Without its protection, would the three of you have fared as well?"

"Aria and Isolde were there as well, and of the five of us, only one had armour," Rowena said. "We defeated the English and none of us were taken hostage or even injured."

Tormod's brows came together. "You were captured by the MacDonalds in a different battle weeks earlier, or have you forgotten that?"

Rowena scowled. "How could I forget with you reminding me every chance you get?"

"I only point it out to help you remember you are but a woman, Rowena. Not a warrior like Isolde, our brother Orrick's wife." Tormod's lips tightened. "Or like the half-fae Aria, our . . . great-aunt? Sister?" He shook his head. "I have no idea what she is to us other than family, but you know what I mean."

She asks us to think of her as a sister, the Grey Lady offered, trying to ease the tension she could no doubt see building between her own children.

"I might not be a warrior like Isolde or Aria, but I can take care of myself." Rowena fisted her hands. Why must they always interfere in her life? "I've proven that I can handle myself when I assisted in protecting both Gwendolyn and Fiona. Or am I only allowed to be strong and independent when it comes to saving your wives?"

"Sister." Alastair slipped from the rock and came towards her. "None of us want anything except your safety. We are not questioning you or your abilities."

Rowena's brows shot up. "That is exactly what you are doing." She stepped back, avoiding the hand that reached for hers.

Rowena, dearest, your brothers are only trying to help. Her mother drifted towards her, arms extended, as though intending to comfort her, before the Grey Lady stopped, remembering she could do nothing of the sort with her ghostly arms.

Rowena felt tears scald the back of her throat. None of them understood her. Perhaps they never would. She held the tears in check as her gaze shifted between her mother and brothers. "Why can't all of you just leave me alone?" Digging her hands into her skirts and lifting them above her ankles, Rowena turned and stomped back towards the castle.

She was angry with them, but also with herself. For in the past few moments, the thought that perhaps they were right had pierced her anger. Were they right? Not about her abilities to keep herself safe, but about waiting for Marcus to return. Was she wasting her life for a man who had left with only the promise that he loved her? She and Marcus had made no serious commitment to each other before he'd left. If Marcus had been so intent on marrying her, why had he not proposed, or asked for Alastair to agree to a betrothal contract?

With her footsteps echoing through the halls of the castle, Rowena made her way to her bedchamber and slammed the door shut. Her breathing was harsh as she leaned back against the wood, forcing herself to calm down when she realised she had only just confirmed what Tormod had claimed. She was acting emotionally, and her behaviour was less than what should be expected of the sister of a great laird.

She pushed away from the door to settle on the bed with a heartfelt sigh. On the morrow, she would have to apologise to her mother, Alastair, and Tormod for her actions unless she wanted them to keep treating her as a fragile bird who could not control her emotions or her behaviour. With another sigh, her thoughts turned to Marcus MacDonald. She did love him even though he was a MacDonald, and she was almost certain he returned that love equally despite the fact she was a MacLeod. Their two clans had always been enemies until the two of them had fallen in love and Marcus had proven his love for her by leaving his MacDonald affiliations behind him.

He'd sacrificed everything for her. That was true love, was it not? And in return, Rowena had promised she would wait for Marcus to come back to her after he made his fortune. Then the two of them could live a comfortable life away from the MacLeods and the MacDonalds.

Rowena stood and moved to her armoire. She opened

the cupboard and pushed aside the gowns that hid the small wooden chest before returning to her bed. She set the box beside her and unhooked the latch, opening the chest to reveal the leather trousers and tunic inside. Six decades ago, Leona MacLeod had worn these same garments into battle with the rest of her clan. The leather had been imbued with fairy magic to protect the wearer from harm. When Fiona had found the garments, the Grey Lady had told her only someone worthy of the fairies' protection could wear them. Fiona had proven she was worthy, but had given the garments to Rowena in case she needed them in the future. If Fiona thought Rowena worthy of wearing the armour, then why didn't her own family?

Rowena stroked the soft leather as a thought occurred to her. Why was she waiting for Marcus to make his fortune so that they might have a future together? Could she not take part in the quest? There were plenty of tales of ships that had gone down along the coast of the Isle of Skye—ships that had been laden with treasure. Or there were tales of treasure buried in the numerous caves along the Isle of Skye's shoreline by smugglers, bootleggers, or pirates. Perhaps, with the protection of the armour, she could find one of those treasure troves and help establish her and Marcus's future herself.

A thump against the shutters broke her thoughts. At first she wondered if it was a bat that had flown into the wooden barrier in the darkness, but the sound came again. She set the chest aside and hurried to the window.

Marcus? Had he returned to her? Warmth flooded her limbs as she threw the shutters aside. The cool night air rushed in as she stared at the rear courtyard below her bedchamber. When no one was there, her gaze lifted to the shore. A single torch shone in the darkness.

A thrill raced through Rowena's blood. Of course Marcus would wait for her along the shoreline. No doubt his ship was anchored offshore and he had taken a boat to get to her as soon as possible. The night was no barrier to their love.

She hesitated at the bedside, considering if she should don the armour she'd retrieved, but decided against it. Marcus was no threat. He would never do anything to harm her.

Her beloved should have presented himself to her brother first, and perhaps that's what he would do in the light of day. Obviously Marcus was willing to toss protocol aside in his haste to see her again. Filled with anticipation, Rowena silently raced down the hallway towards the stairs, then outside and down the pathway towards the sea gate. Throwing the gate aside, she knew she had to hurry before the guards on the tower noticed the torch and came to investigate. While Alastair had given her and Marcus his blessing to marry eventually, Marcus was still a MacDonald and not yet accepted by all within the castle walls.

On the beach, Rowena scrambled over the rocks in the

darkness, towards the torch. The flame hissed, sending a spray of red-gold sparks into the night air. She shivered, not from cold but from the fact that Marcus was nowhere in sight.

"Marcus? Is that you?" The *Na Fir-Chlis* were beautiful, but they did nothing to illuminate the shoreline before her. Rowena grabbed the torch and held it before her. She could see nothing but knew someone was there. Why didn't Marcus reveal himself? "I've been waiting for you every night. I prayed for your safety, and your speedy return. I missed you," she said, hoping he was simply hesitating because of the need to judge her steadfastness in his absence. "Marcus, please show yourself. I want nothing more than to hold you in my arms."

At her words, a shadow separated itself from the darkness. Even though she could not yet see a face, she could tell the shape was that of a male. Although this shape was shorter and more lean than the man she loved.

"Who are you?" she asked, trying to keep her sudden fear from her voice.

Without hesitation, the man stepped into the circle of the torchlight. *Bryce.* Marcus's cousin, and her one-time attacker when she'd been imprisoned at the seat of the MacDonald clan, Monkstadt House.

"I can see in your eyes that you are surprised to see me." Bryce's dark gaze locked on hers.

She couldn't read his expression, but after their last

struggle at the MacDonald stronghold when she'd hit Bryce on the head, allowing her to escape, she was certain he'd be angry. "Why are you here?" She clutched the torch she'd retrieved a moment earlier, using it as a shield. Though not a true weapon, the flames offered her a certain amount of protection. She groaned inwardly. Why had she not taken a moment to don the leather tunic and trousers she'd retrieved from her armoire?

"I came to claim a prize that has eluded me for months." His tone was suddenly fierce.

Rowena forced herself not to react, though she shivered inside as she faced him. Bryce had tried to force himself on her once already in an attempt to ruin her before she could wed Marcus. Was that his intent now?

Bryce lifted his hand and levelled a pistol at her. "You do not have to worry about me having my way with you. At least not in the near future. I have other plans for you."

Her torch was no match for a bullet, yet she waved the torch at him, forcing Bryce to take a step back. "I will not surrender to you without a fight."

He shrugged. "I expected as much." With a nod of his head, two men appeared out of the darkness. One kicked the torch out of her hands and sent her reeling backwards.

The torch dropped to the rocky beach but before she hit the rocks, she was pulled upright by a beefy hand on her arm. "Nay," she cried as she was jerked towards a solid chest.

The hilt of the second man's sword bit into her hip. He

dug his fingers into the flesh of her arm as he smiled a wicked smile. "What are we gonna do with her now?"

"We are going to take her back to our lair and wait for my cousin to arrive." Bryce's voice hardened on the last words.

Instead of fear, hope leapt inside Rowena. "Marcus is here? He's returned?" She'd sensed his nearness over the past few days. Why had she not listened to her brothers and her mother? They had been right to be concerned for her safety outside of the castle walls. She opened her mouth to scream, but Bryce stepped closer, placing the gun against her chest.

"No histrionics, or I'll shoot you here and now." His eyes locked on hers. There was a shadow of desperation lurking in his dark eyes.

Instead of screaming, Rowena stared down at the pistol pressed against where her heart thundered in her chest. Bryce wanted something from her and from Marcus. Until he got whatever it was, he wasn't going to harm her. The thought kept her from total panic. With an effort she drew a breath and tried to think of what to do—how to wrest the gun away from him and break free from the big oaf who held her captive—but her brain couldn't focus on anything other than the fact that Marcus had returned.

Drawing in a breath, trying desperately to think, she attempted to shake off the iron grip on her arm, without success. "Let me go. Marcus will kill you if you harm me."

"I don't want to harm you, not unless you force me to do

so. I want something far more precious than your feminine attributes, and I intend to use you to extort it from my cousin." An expression of satisfaction lent brief animation to his features.

She lifted her chin, suddenly understanding. "You want his newfound wealth."

"My cousin has everything. The strength of a new clan, you, and most likely a fortune from his endeavours on the high seas," Bryce said in a tightly controlled voice. Beneath the words she could hear his fury.

Truly puzzled by his logic, she shook her head. "How could you know anything about a fortune? Marcus has yet to return."

Bryce's lips curled. "I know my cousin. He succeeds at everything. And he *has* returned. I saw his ship anchoring off Point Neist early this afternoon."

Rowena staggered on her feet. Marcus had not come for her immediately. Her throat constricted even as she forced herself to breathe. The pain of that betrayal welled and swelled inside her.

A shout from the tower jolted Rowena back to the moment. Someone on the tower had seen the torchlight or motion on the shoreline below and had sounded an alarm.

"Hellfire," Bryce muttered under his breath. He moved the pistol from her chest. "We must head to the trees." The second man came forward to grasp her other arm. With the pistol, Bryce motioned Rowena forward. When she didn't move, the giant men attached to her arms dragged her towards the trees.

She strained her ears to listen for the footsteps of the guards coming down the passageway to the sea gate. The men were running, but they would never reach the shoreline before the three of them disappeared into the trees.

"Hurry up." Bryce's pistol dug into her side as the two men swept her forward.

A chill slid through her at the touch of cold metal through her gown. They leapt over the stream that fed Loch Dunvegan and were at the edge of the treeline when Rowena wrenched back, surprising her captors. She broke free of their grasp and pulled away from the cold muzzle of the pistol, praying Bryce wouldn't pull the trigger. "Help!" She looked for dark figures on the shoreline, but the guards had yet to arrive through the sea gate. Desperate to let them know she had been taken, she redoubled her volume. "*Help!*"

"Damn you," Bryce snarled as something hard hit her head.

She swayed as the world swirled before her. Before she could catch herself, she was lifted off her feet and tossed over the back of a horse. Her head pounded as she collapsed against the animal's warm coat. A heartbeat later, Bryce mounted behind her and none too gently pulled her upright to lean against his chest. The horse lurched forward. She opened her eyes briefly but couldn't focus her senses enough to stop the world from spinning.

Bryce held her tight as he rummaged in his saddlebag for something. "I'd hoped this wouldn't be necessary, but I underestimated you yet again. That will be the last time. I promise you."

He leaned closer. A waft of sweetness reached her, then intensified into a suffocating, cloying smell. A cloth clamped over her nose and mouth.

Rowena struggled, trying desperately to turn her head away from the smell, away from the grasp Bryce had over her. She held her breath as she continued to struggle until her body rebelled, drawing a breath of the cloying concoction.

As darkness closed in, a single desperate sob escaped her. Her field of vision narrowed to blackness. Her last conscious thoughts were that she had done exactly what her brothers had feared. She'd failed to protect herself. Now she was alone with no one to help her. Not even Marcus. He hadn't come for her. He had deserted her and left her in the hands of his cousin. A man who would exploit her for his own gain.

CHAPTER THREE

MARCUS MACDONALD'S HAND tightened on the tiller as the coastline of Scotland's Neist Point came into view. The craggy basalt cliffs with their verdant green tops usually brought a sense of peace when he gazed upon them, but not this evening. With the sun setting behind him, Marcus ordered that the sails be lowered and the ropes secured. He and his men would anchor offshore overnight and proceed to Dunvegan on the morrow. Marcus needed a few hours more to decide how to proceed even though he'd been thinking about this very moment for the past six months.

"You are returning to Dunvegan a wealthy man." Eck came to stand at the railing, leaning against it as though he had not a care in the world.

"As are you." Marcus released his grip on the tiller as the men set the anchor.

"Are you not happy to see your sweet Rowena once more?" Eck arched a brow.

Marcus frowned. "I've been away from Dunvegan for six months. The man who has returned is a different man than the one who left."

"Granted we endured hardship, but we are better men for all that we suffered."

"Are we?" Marcus had started his journey intent on gaining his fortune through battle, as he'd done his whole life as a part of the MacDonald clan. Instead, he'd been handed a gift by a stranger, yet that gift had come with a steep price.

"We lost several men," Eck acknowledged.

"Several men?" Marcus drew a deep breath of the salt-laden air, allowing it to calm him as it had over the past weeks when he'd thought of the loss of life his crew had endured. To die in battle was an honourable way to die. To die treasure hunting seemed reckless and foolhardy. The gold and silver they'd retrieved from a hellish grave was forever etched with the blood of those they'd lost. "We left with seven-and-seventy men and returned with only five-and-forty. Two-and-thirty men sacrificed their lives while hunting for that damn treasure."

"What would you have done differently?" Eck straightened. "Left Jacob Thorne to die in a watery grave along with his men? To never learn about not one but two treasures that were ours for the taking?"

Marcus gazed out at the water. "Perhaps I never should have left on this tragic journey at all. I always imagined us fighting for what we would gain, to earn it with grit and honour, not to take advantage of those around us." Over the past few months, he'd written letters to the families the dead crew members had left behind, praying the funds he and his men had recovered would somehow make up for the losses these families would endure. Now that they had reached shore, Marcus would have to deliver those letters along with a portion of the treasure. He would relive the loss of his men over again as he stared into the eyes of the dead men's parents, widows, and children.

During many a sleepless night he'd wondered if building a future life with Rowena had been worth the sacrifice. She hadn't forced him on this adventure, but he never would have felt the need to go if it wasn't for her. Rowena MacLeod was used to a certain elaborate lifestyle. In order to keep her comfortable in her current way of life as his bride, she had cost him two-and-thirty men.

"You blame the girl, don't you?" Eck asked as though reading Marcus's thoughts. The two of them had grown close over their months at sea.

"It's hard not to. She is the reason we left Scotland to pursue our fortunes." Pressing his lips into a hard thin line, Marcus turned away from Eck. "I can't help but wonder if the crazy emotions I shared with Rowena were even real, or just a bright flame of bad judgement that snuffed out shortly after we left." He had gone weeks without thinking about her once. Should he take that as a sign?

Thank heaven her brother, Alastair, had refused to allow them to sign a betrothal agreement before Marcus had left, otherwise there would be no other way forward. Perhaps

Rowena had moved on with her life during his absence. The thought brought with it a flicker of bittersweet hope.

"I can read in your eyes that you are planning and plotting. Don't be an arse. That girl is a treasure all on her own. I would think twice before you throw her away, my friend."

At Eck's harsh words Marcus turned back. "You find me so easy to read?"

"After six months at your side, aye," Eck said dryly. "But then again, if you toss her aside, she might need a shoulder to cry on. Perhaps I will volunteer for that role."

Marcus scowled. "You wouldn't dare."

Eck shrugged. "If you don't want her . . ."

"Now who's being an arse?" Marcus asked, as a sense of reassurance came over him at the jealousy that flashed hot and quick at Eck's suggestion. If he didn't still care about Rowena, he wouldn't feel that way. Would he?

"All the gold in the world cannot buy you happiness," Eck said. "Think long and hard before you toss Rowena aside."

Marcus's gaze sifted to the coastline that would lead him back to Dunvegan and Rowena tomorrow. "That's just it. I don't know if it was true happiness I felt when I was with Rowena all those months ago."

"Then seeing her again should either affirm what you felt was real or expose the fact it was not."

Marcus found he was experiencing a multitude of wild emotions that took him completely off guard. Anger and frustration battled with an odd sense of guilt. "You make it sound so simple." But he had to acknowledge that Eck was right. One look would help Marcus reconcile the image of the woman his mind had conjured over the many months with the flesh-and-blood woman he would see on the morrow.

AT THE CALL to arms that sounded from above, Alastair swung his leg over the side of the bed, leaving his pregnant wife, Gwendolyn, behind. He sprang to his feet, donned his shirt, then quickly folded and secured his tartan about his waist with a leather belt. Shoving his feet into his boots and securing his scabbard about his waist, Alastair bolted for the door. He raced down the stairs, heading for the courtyard. They hadn't had an emergency at the castle for months. What could possibly be happening now?

His footsteps slowed as he pushed out the castle door and emerged into the courtyard. Torches and lanterns illuminated the courtyard as several guardsmen gathered and the horses were brought out from the stable saddled and ready. At the sight of him, the captain of the guard hurried towards Alastair. "Are we under attack?"

Graeme shook his head. "Worse. The tower guards saw three men abduct Rowena from along the shoreline."

"Hellfire!" Alastair's sense of unease gave way to fear.

"Do we know who they were?" His hand fell to his sword.

"They wore dark clothing and hoods to cover their faces," Graeme replied. "Not that the tower guards could have recognised them from that distance in the dark."

A shuffling came from the doorway as Tormod MacLeod erupted into the courtyard dressed for battle with his *clai'mor* at his back, a broadsword at his hip, and a pistol tucked into his belt. "What is it? What's wrong?"

Callum emerged right behind his older brother. "Are we going into battle?"

"Not battle," Alastair said. "On a search. Someone has abducted our sister."

"Who would do such a thing?" Callum asked in shocked disbelief.

Tormod's features clouded. "Any one of our enemies."

Alastair headed for his horse. Graeme, Tormod, and Callum mounted as well. "Which direction did they head?"

The guardsmen took their saddles, and the gatekeeper opened the portcullis. "To the east," Graeme said, sitting forward on his horse, ready to signal the guards who were mounted to ride out.

"It doesn't mean they will maintain that course," Alastair said with a frown as his gaze passed between his brothers and his friend. "We should divide the guardsmen, and each of us will lead a group in a different direction."

"Who will guard the castle?" Callum asked.

"Our fairy sister, Aria," Alastair replied. "She has proven

she is more than capable with the help of the guards we will leave behind."

With the safety of the castle having been determined, Graeme efficiently divided up the guardsmen then returned to where the MacLeod brothers waited. "Alastair, you head east. Tormod, go to the west. Callum, you should lead a group to the south, and I'll head north. Three men should be no challenge for any of us but be on guard for anything. If these men were clever, they would have anticipated a large response from the MacLeods. They may have set traps."

Alastair nodded. "May luck guide us all until our sister is safely returned."

Tormod, Callum, and Graeme all brought a fist to their chests before they each rode into the waiting darkness beyond the castle gate.

ROWENA OPENED HER eyes. Darkness surrounded her as she tried to raise her hands to brush her hair from her face, only to find her wrists were bound. Her feet as well. She lay on her side atop something hard and cold. As she shifted her body in an effort to assess where she was, the scent of soil and lichens came to her. She was on the ground.

She cast her gaze about her, trying to determine if Bryce or her other two attackers were near, but was forced to close her eyes as whatever Bryce had used to drug her had left her dizzy and nauseated. She lay there for several long moments, forcing herself to breathe deeply until the sensation ebbed. The silence around her brought her a sense of comfort. Surely if anyone else was present, she would hear something.

What did Bryce have planned for her? He'd tried to force himself on her at their last meeting, but she and Fiona's father had stopped him short of his goal. Would he try such a thing again? If he meant to rape her or even kill her, it would have been easy enough to do while she was senseless. Nay, he wanted her alive and unspoiled, at least for the moment, and the reason had something to do with Marcus.

The only scenario that made any sense was that Bryce would hold her hostage and demand ransom from Marcus now that he had returned for her. A roaring filled Rowena's ears at the thought that Marcus hadn't come for her immediately. What did that mean? Bryce had only said he'd seen Marcus's ship, not the man himself. Had Marcus been killed or injured during his voyage?

Rowena drew a ragged breath as a sense of impending loss swamped her. With her next breath, she forced the thought away. Marcus lived; she knew it. If he had died, she would feel it in the depths of her soul. With the same certainty, she told herself that Marcus would come for her now. Fate might have sent them in two different directions, but she did not doubt his devotion to her. There was a reasonable explanation why he had not come to her immediately upon his return.

Despite all that, Marcus would know she needed saving and he would come for her. She was absolutely certain of that. Until he could find her, she had to help herself. Never would she allow Bryce to take away the future she'd planned and waited for six long months to achieve.

Her senses returning to normal once more, Rowena opened her eyes. Darkness still pervaded the space she occupied, yet even without light she could see a few feet in front of her. She was in a room of some sort with an earthen floor. Silencing her thoughts, she listened. Beyond whatever walls contained her, she could hear male voices. What they said, she couldn't make out. But she also noted the sound of water softly lapping against a shoreline in the distance and the unmistakable bark of seals she heard every night while watching the horizon for Marcus's ship. Loch Dunvegan was home to many harbour seals. Did that mean Bryce hadn't taken her far from home?

Determined to be free of her restraints, Rowena straightened her legs only to discover she could move her ankles only a few fingers' length apart. Her hands she could not separate at all. They were tied palm to palm with the knot on the outside of her right hand. She tried to bend towards her hands, intent on using her teeth to loosen the knot, when the door of the chamber opened and Bryce stepped inside. In one hand he held a lantern, in the other a chair.

Yellow-gold light spilled through the chamber, revealing a small cottage. The only building of the sort near the loch were crofters' cottages that sat farther up the coastline from Dunvegan. But this cottage was not made of wattle and daub as those were. This one was constructed of oak. She had no time to further her observations as Bryce dropped the chair and rushed towards her.

"What are you doing?" He yanked her to her feet, then reclaimed the chair and shoved her onto it. He set the lantern down and grabbed another length of rope that waited by the door. Rowena writhed and bucked against the chair as he held her pressed against it, but Bryce's strength out-matched hers. Eventually he was able to wind the rope about her chest, securing it behind her, making escape nearly impossible.

"Where am I?" she demanded.

He stepped back and appraised her through slitted lids. "You are in the perfect hiding place. Close to your family but in a place they will never think to look for you."

Rowena searched her memory for locations that had a wooden hut close to Dunvegan but could think of no such place. As she frowned, Bryce's smile increased.

"You are on *Gairbh Eilein*."

Rowena started at the revelation, then just as quickly hid her surprise. "The rocky, seal isle in the loch?" The small isle was visible from the castle's rear courtyard and towers. Bryce might have successfully abducted her, but his choice of hideout would be discovered by her brothers in no time at all.

"They will never find you," Bryce mocked. "This hunting hide hasn't been used in years and its location on the north-eastern shore makes it impossible to see from Dunvegan."

Rowena scowled. Not if she set it on fire. Which she intended to do the first chance she got.

"No one is coming to rescue you. Not even Marcus, who has no idea this place even exists."

Her anger flared at the suggestion that he could outsmart his own cousin and her brothers. "You won't get away with this. I'll scream and keep screaming until someone hears me."

"One sound out of you and I'll kill you first, and then Marcus. I'll take everything he has earned on his voyage as my own." The dark look in Bryce's eyes and the dagger at his belt confirmed his words were no empty threat.

Rowena swallowed roughly and forced her panicked wits aside. She did not want to die now that Marcus had finally returned home. "I won't scream."

"Clever girl."

"What happens next?" she asked, once more testing the rope at her wrists, hoping she'd eased the knot with her teeth in the brief moment she'd tried, but the knot held firm.

"We wait for Marcus to come to Dunvegan in search of you. When he does, he will receive a note requesting a ransom be paid for your safe return."

Rowena's heart clogged her throat. He hadn't come for

her when she thought he would. "What if he refuses to pay the ransom?"

Bryce reached for his dagger and brought it to rest against her chest, right above her heart. "Then I'll have no choice but to take from him what at one time he could not live without." Bryce's dagger moved from her chest. He tugged the ends of her hair near her shoulder and sliced off a handful. "I'll need this as proof that I have you." He removed a kerchief from his sporran and placed the hair upon the cloth before folding it again and returning it to the pouch.

Rowena's earlier certainty that Marcus would come for her faltered. Her fingers clenched and released as she fought the sense of abandonment that threatened to choke her. Her three brothers had forsaken her when they'd left home five years ago. Even her own parents had deserted her. Her father after he had injured his head in a battle and had become a cruel, abusive stranger. Her mother when she had died due to her father's brutality. And now Marcus would neglect her as well.

Rowena swallowed roughly, halting the thought before it could fully form. Marcus had not abandoned her yet. There was still hope that he was alive and that he would come for her. She lifted her chin and met Bryce's steely gaze. "Marcus will pay the ransom."

"You'd better hope he does, or tonight could be your last night upon this earth."

Despite the fact that time was running out for her, Rowena held her head high. Marcus would either pay the ransom or she would have to find some way to escape.

There was no other choice.

CHAPTER FOUR

THE EARLY MORNING sunshine had yet to burn through the mist that gathered in pockets along the shores of Dunvegan Castle. Marcus and seven other men brought their boat to a stop in the shallow surf. "Wait for me here," Marcus called to his men as they lifted the oars. "This shouldn't take long." As he jumped into the water and made his way to the rocky beach, he went over in his mind what he would say to Rowena.

He looked up and down the shoreline, half expecting to see her waiting for him. When he'd left her six months ago, she'd stood on this very beach with tears in her eyes. Had he expected his return to be met with the same emotion? Irritation shot through him at her absence, until he reminded himself he should be pleased at this turn of events.

Perhaps she had changed her mind about him. If she had, it would make his uncomfortable task that much easier. He'd decided late into the night that he would be honest with Rowena. He would tell her his duty to his men's families took precedence over any attachment they had, and he would admit that his feelings had changed while he'd been away at sea.

He wasn't expecting hysterics from Rowena at his confession. She wasn't that kind of woman. Now he wondered if she would be troubled at all to learn about his change of heart. Forcing his expectations aside, Marcus made his way over the wet, algae-covered rocks only to stop a heartbeat later, when a man, dressed in a black tunic and breeches, stepped out of the natural outcropping of the large basalt rock on which Dunvegan Castle perched. He recognised the man immediately as his cousin, Bryce.

"Why are you here?" Marcus snapped. His cousin was the last person he'd expected to greet him upon his return.

Bryce laughed, the sound of the sea muting most of it. "I can see you running through every scenario of my presence here in your eyes. You always made it so easy to read your thoughts, dear cousin."

"Where are Alastair, Tormod, or Orrick?" Why hadn't the MacLeod brothers been the ones to challenge him on their beach? "Where's Rowena?" Marcus's gaze went over Bryce's head to the golden stones of Dunvegan Castle. No guards perched on the towers, and no sound came from the rear courtyard overhead.

Uncertainty tore through him. Something had happened. "What aren't you telling me?"

"Only a hundred or so men remain at Dunvegan. The rest have gone off in search of your dear Rowena." Bryce smiled, looking absurdly pleased with himself.

"What did you do?" Marcus's eyes narrowed as he grabbed Bryce's throat.

"Don't harm me," Bryce rasped, "or you'll never see the girl again."

Rowena. He was talking about Rowena. Marcus loosened his grip but did not remove his hand.

Bryce stretched his neck and took a deep breath of air before smiling. "It's truly a brilliant plan. I kidnapped Rowena and have hidden her where you or her brothers will never find her unless you pay me a ransom for her return."

"Why?" The horror of Bryce's words pierced Marcus's brain. "What is this really about, Bryce? Are you angry that I turned my back on the MacDonald clan? On you? If so, take your hostilities out on me."

"I intend to." His smile turned sinister. "I know you have returned to Scotland a wealthy man, and I want every piece of that treasure or I will kill your lovely bride."

Marcus forced Bryce away from him with so much force that his cousin nearly fell backwards as he stumbled to catch himself. "You never change, Bryce. You were always jealous of what others had, especially me. Yet you were never willing to work for anything yourself."

Bryce rubbed his neck. "I'm not like you, Cousin. I've never been good with a sword, because no one wanted to train me. I'm not supported by our clan as you always were, but then you were the one who betrayed the MacDonalds, fighting for the MacLeods instead."

"If you weren't so irritating, you might have had those things."

Bryce scowled. "Don't act all high and mighty with me. The tables have turned. You're the one who will suffer now because I've taken the woman you love from you and will not return her unless you give me your treasure."

While Marcus was concerned for Rowena's safety, he didn't think his cousin had it in him to kill the woman if he really did have her. "How do I know you are telling me the truth? There are many reasons for the MacLeods to be absent from Dunvegan."

Bryce reached inside his sporran and brought forth a kerchief that contained a swath of dark brown hair. "Is this enough proof? Or should I bring you one of her fingers instead?"

The dark brown hair bordered on the edge of black, yet it glistened in the morning sun much the same way it had when he'd walked with Rowena on this very beach, dreaming of the future they would share. Regardless of this proof, Marcus could not do what Bryce wanted. Though fifty per cent of the treasure was his to take as captain of the ship, he would only keep a small portion of that. The remaining treasure would go to the families of every man who had died in its recovery. "I have no treasure to offer you."

"How can that be?" For a moment an expression of uneasiness crossed Bryce's face.

"What we recovered is not mine to give."

"That's ridiculous. You found treasure. How can it not be yours?" Bryce's gaze bored into Marcus's. "Will you pay the ransom or not?"

"I will not."

Bryce's face reddened. "I'm not playing with you, Cousin, if that's what you think."

"I'm not toying with you either. I cannot pay the ransom."

A flicker of impatience passed over Bryce's face. "Do you smell blood, Cousin? Because if you cannot, then you soon will. I—" His words cut off at the sound of horse's hooves on the packed earth of the front courtyard above them.

Marcus's gaze shifted to the castle. "Sounds like some of the MacLeods have returned. Perhaps you'd like to approach one of Rowena's brothers with your offer?" Marcus returned his gaze to his cousin and almost smiled as the colour drained from Bryce's face.

Bryce backed away, heading towards the treeline. "I'll give you until sundown tomorrow to change your mind or I will kill the girl."

Marcus started after his cousin but as soon as Bryce reached the trees he leapt onto the back of a waiting horse, disappearing into the thick foliage. Marcus slowed from a run then stopped. He could not follow his cousin on foot, and even if he followed the coastline in his boat, he could not track his cousin if he went inland. Instead, he signalled his men to leave the boat and follow him. Marcus was left with no other choice than to climb the embankment to the front gates of Dunvegan. He would inform Rowena's family that his cousin had abducted her and which direction Bryce had gone.

Together, the eight men started their climb. Marcus remained silent, pressing his lips together in thought. There wasn't much that could rattle him after all he'd been through in the last few months, but facing any one of Rowena's older brothers suddenly made risking his life for a sunken treasure seem like child's play. The MacLeod brothers were a force to be reckoned with when one of their own was in trouble or betrayed.

MORNING LIGHT SEEPED under the doorway of the hunting hide as Rowena stretched her stiff muscles. She'd dozed off a few times during the night while she'd been slowly working to loosen the ropes that bound her. Her captors had left her alone during the night. No doubt the ropes at her chest, hands, and feet made them think there was no way for her to escape.

What they didn't know was that as Bryce had tied the rope about her chest, she'd filled her lungs with air, increasing her girth so when she breathed out, the ropes were not as tight as he thought they were.

She'd spent the better part of the night wiggling her torso, hands, and arms, slowly stretching the rope. Though red abrasions marred her wrists, she'd worked the rope loose enough so that with one more tug downward, she slipped one hand free.

Elation shot through Rowena as she quickly tossed the rope off her other hand and went to work on the knot at her chest. It didn't take long to free herself after all her loosening over the night. All that remained was the knot at her ankles.

Her heart leapt to her throat at the sound of footsteps and muffled voices outside her door. Her fingers worked the knot until finally she felt it give, then hurried to untangle the rest. When she was finally free, she stood on unsteady legs and looked about the hunting blind for somewhere to hide.

The single room had no furnishings and no windows. Since there was no other option, she'd have to fight her way to freedom. She did not wear the fairy garments of her ancestor, but her mother had told Rowena that in order to wear the garments successfully a bit of fairy magic had to flow in her blood. Rowena hoped that bit of magic might help her now as she fought for her life.

As the latch on the door moved down, Rowena gripped the chair and moved closer to the door. Her only chance would be to take the men by surprise, then slip past them and run faster than she ever had in her life.

As the door opened slightly, she widened her stance and brought the chair up over her head. Bryce's red hair was the first thing she saw. Using all her strength, she brought the chair down, hard. Bryce crumpled to the floor. The two men behind him charged into the chamber, drawing their daggers. The men expected another attack from overhead, so instead Rowena aimed for their legs with the back of the chair, sending them off balance one after the other. She threw the chair aside and darted out the door.

She had no idea where she was on the small isle, but it didn't matter. Any direction she ran would eventually take her to the water and her only chance for escape. Blood pounded in her ears and the harsh sound of her breath filled the morning air as she raced across the rocky terrain. There were no trees to hide her, only sea grass that made the path before her even more treacherous because she could not see the ragged rocks beneath. Leaping from one rock to the next, she kept up her rapid pace despite the danger.

Behind her she heard a shout then Bryce's roar of fury. Rowena glanced back over her shoulder. Her stomach twisted into a knot. Bryce and his two henchmen chased her. *Merciful heavens.* They were going to catch her. The thought sent prickles along her skin.

She returned her gaze to the path ahead and increased her focus on the swiftest route across the ragged rocks. The stomping sounds behind her grew closer. What would they do if they caught her? This time instead of tying her to a chair, they might torture and then murder her.

The thought fuelled her legs to move faster. She could see the waterline as well as nearly fifty harbour seals ahead, basking in the morning sunshine. She forced herself to breathe evenly as she battled against the fear rising in her throat. She had been raised to be wary of the seals. All the MacLeod children had grown up hearing fairy stories, including those featuring selkies who took the form of seals during the daylight hours.

Holding her fear in check, she kept up her rapid pace, despite the slippery surface of rocks covered by algae and kelp. At Rowena's presence, the seals near her undulated towards the water, making barely a sound as they disappeared below the surface.

"You cannot escape me. Surrender." Bryce's words ground out with wrath.

Rowena's heart hammered at her breastbone. At the water's edge she hesitated. What would the seals do to her as she swam back towards the castle? A quick glance over her shoulder showed Bryce nearly upon her. He wore the promise of death on his face. Without another thought, she dove into the cool water of the loch, taking her chances amongst the seals.

"BLOODY HELL!" THE stupid girl had tricked him. Bryce came to a sudden stop at the edge of the water and turned to his men. "Go in after her."

Rabbie and Gus simply stared at him with horror on

their faces. "We canna swim. Ye go after her," Rabbie said.

The muscles of Bryce's back tightened as he fisted his hands at his sides, watching Rowena's bobbing head grow farther away from him. He'd never learned to swim. The one time he had tried, he'd sunk to the bottom of the loch before his father could pull him back to the surface. It had felt like he'd coughed water from his lungs for days. Bryce had never been brave enough to try again.

"To the boat," he ordered. "Hurry. If she gets away, one of you will pay for her loss." The iciness of his words sent the men into a faster pace.

Bryce had hidden the small boat in a narrow cove that would take several minutes to reach on foot. It would be a miracle if they could get to the boat and overcome Rowena before she made it to shore. But then again, if they got close enough, he could always shoot her with his pistol. She deserved to die for ruining his plans. His cousin deserved to lose not only the woman, but also everything he held dear for refusing to pay the ransom Bryce had demanded.

The two of them would get what they deserved. One way or another.

CHAPTER FIVE

MARCUS STOOD BEFORE the massive gates of Dunvegan. He'd been here many times before as an enemy of the MacLeods. Yet this time when the gatekeeper saw him, he was admitted without question since Marcus had battled with the MacLeods against his own clan.

Had it only been six months ago that he'd betrayed his own people for Rowena? He wasn't sorry he'd left most of his kin behind, because his mother and father had been allowed to come live at Dunvegan while Marcus had left.

At least that had been the plan. Now six months later, everything was different. He was no longer a man in love. He was a traitor to his clan. And truly, he had no notion if he was better off financially than the day he'd left. Until he parcelled out the treasure to the families of the men he'd lost, he wouldn't know what remained. He could still be a wealthy man, or he might be a privateer with only a ship to his name.

As Marcus walked across the drawbridge, he thought about his parents. What would happen to them when he broke things off with Rowena? He could always take them with him on *The Cliodna* until he paid his debts to his lost men, then the three of them could determine a new future together, perhaps in Glasgow where one's clan affiliation mattered far less than it did in the Highlands.

Marcus frowned. He wasn't certain he could abandon the Highlands with as much ease as Rowena. War was coming. It was only a matter of time before either the neighbouring clans or the English army clashed with the Highlanders. Pushing his thoughts aside, Marcus proceeded into the courtyard where he was met by Alastair.

Alastair came forward with a smile. "Marcus. Glad we are to see you safely back amongst us. When did you return? We did not see your ship."

"*The Cliodna* is anchored off Neist Point. My men and I came by boat to your shore." Marcus nodded to the men following him into the courtyard. "I came as soon as I was able." It wasn't a lie, but an evasion of the truth.

"'Tis good you are back." Alastair's smile slipped. "There is no easy way to say this. Rowena has been kidnapped. My brothers are out searching for her. My men and I returned when several of our horses picked up rocks in their hooves. We think whoever took Rowena set a trap for us. As soon as new horses are saddled, we'll ride out again. Join us."

Marcus swallowed as all eyes in the courtyard turned to him. "My cousin, Bryce, kidnapped your sister. He was waiting for me on the shoreline when I arrived just now."

"What did the MacDonald say to you?" Alastair demanded, his features suddenly hard.

"He told me Rowena is in a place none of us would ever find." Lowering his gaze slightly, Marcus continued, "Bryce demanded I pay a ransom for her return."

Alastair nodded. "You agreed to these terms."

"I refused."

"You refused?" The last word was drawn out as Alastair's fists became as tight as his scowl. "I thought you loved Rowena?"

Instinct screamed for Marcus to step back, away from the danger, but he kept himself straight, drawing on the courage he'd gained over the past several months. "I cannot offer Bryce something that is not mine to give."

The anger on Alastair's face dropped to surprise. "You found treasure, did you?"

"And lost two-and-thirty men in the process. I cannot do anything with my share of the treasure until I make settlements to all the families those men left behind."

Alastair's fists relaxed. "That is admirable. Though I dare say that doesn't help Rowena. What did Bryce demand? Would he accept payment from the MacLeods instead?"

"He did not remain long enough for me to ask him."

"Then you saw him leave?"

"He is heading west."

Alastair turned and strode towards the closest horse, throwing himself up in the saddle. "Grab a horse and let's go after him." To his men he said, "Those with horses come with us. The rest stay here and monitor the shoreline."

Marcus mounted, then turned to his men. "Stay here. Keep watch with the MacLeods."

Alastair and Marcus headed for the gate when a young, white-haired woman waved her hands above her head from the tower above, signalling them to stop. "A swimmer approaches along the shoreline."

Alastair was off his horse in a heartbeat. As soon as his feet hit the ground, he ran to the sea gate. Marcus followed. The laird threw the gate open, pounded across the rocky beach, and into the water just as the swimmer approached.

Instead of watching the laird as he apprehended whoever dared to approach the castle, Marcus's gaze lifted to a boat in the distance with three men inside. Bryce's unmistakable red hair shone like a beacon. His cousin held a pistol aimed at the swimmer's back as the sodden mass started to rise from the water. At the threat of danger, Marcus raced into the water. "Get down!" he yelled at Alastair as Marcus crashed into the creature chest first, taking the two of them below the water.

He caught the bedraggled mass, hauling the creature to him. Marcus nearly drew in a lungful of water when instead of hard muscle as he'd expected, softness pressed into his chest. *A woman?*

When he was certain he'd foiled Bryce's shot, Marcus broke the water's surface, taking the woman with him. His gaze returned to where Bryce's boat had been. He and his men were rowing away. "This isn't over, Cousin," Bryce yelled, his teeth showing as his mouth pulled back in a snarl.

The woman in his arms pushed against his chest, forcing Marcus to release his hold. She stood in the waist-deep water and pushed the wet hair from her face.

Marcus startled. *Rowena.*

Her sodden dark gown pressed against her body, revealing every nuance of her soft curves. Her hair, which usually a glory of lustrous dark brown silk, was a mass of disarray with kelp sticking out at odd angles. Her pink lips were slightly parted, and her hazel eyes filled with annoyance that quickly turned to joy.

"Marcus. You came back for me." She threw herself into his arms.

He brought his hands up to caress her back, the muscles in his belly knotting as the scent of heather and sunshine radiated from her skin. Six months away suddenly seemed like only yesterday as a need as strong as it had ever been washed over him. He inhaled sharply at its impact. How could he have forgotten his body's response to this woman when he held her in his arms?

He closed his eyes and allowed himself this one small indulgence before he set her from him. His response mattered not. He still had to break things off with her because he didn't want to make Rowena wait any longer while he went off to find the families of his men. He suspected that task could take many months, if not years. It was a task he had to accomplish without Rowena at his side. The thought stung, but instead of pushing away the pain he latched on to it. The discomfort would help him recall his goals when he remembered the feel of her body wrapped in his arms.

⁓

HEAT SURROUNDED HER, invading her senses, piercing the heavy veil of loneliness that had held her in its grasp for the past six months. Then the heat vanished as Marcus released her.

Rowena's gaze flew to Marcus's face. How many lonely nights had she lain awake waiting for his return, wondering what had happened to him, longing for him to be by her side? His dark eyes met hers and she saw surprise, pain, then the most gut-wrenching emotion of all, apathy.

Tightness gripped her chest, making it hard to breathe. "What's wrong? What is it?"

Alastair rose up from the water beside them, interrupting the moment. After checking to see the danger was past, he looped his hand about her waist, guiding her back to the beach. "Are you well? We know Bryce MacDonald kidnapped you."

"I am unharmed. Bryce held me hostage on *Gairbh Eilein*."

Alastair gazed over his shoulder to the isle in the distance. "None of us thought to look for you there."

"That's what Bryce expected," Rowena said as the three of them broke through the surf to stand on the shoreline, soft waves lapping at their feet.

"How did you escape?"

Rowena smiled. "My brothers are not the only clever ones in this family." Her smile slipped a heartbeat later. "Though I must admit even though I am a strong swimmer, I had difficulty in the currents. That's when I had a little help making it to shore."

Alastair's brows came together. "What do you mean?"

Rowena pursed her lips. "You know how mother always warned us about getting too close to the seals?"

He nodded, though confusion filled his dark eyes. "Did they somehow help you escape?"

"It was the strangest thing. The light seals with dark speckles surrounded me, pulling me deeper. I couldn't break free and pull myself back to the surface for air. Then, out of nowhere, the dark seals with light spots attacked the lighter ones and lifted me to the surface. They propelled me towards the beach, putting themselves between me and Bryce's boat when it came after us. I hardly know what to think."

Alastair frowned. "I'm sure mother will have an opinion on the matter. Nevertheless, I am so grateful you were not harmed by Bryce or the seals. Now that you are back, there is no need to figure out how to pay the ransom that Marcus would not."

Rowena's breath hitched as she turned to Marcus. "You

refused to pay the ransom?"

Marcus held out his hand. "Come, let us return you to the castle and allow you to clean up and eat something, then we will talk."

She knew her hair was a tousled mess, her clothes were limp and drenched with water, but even so she hesitated, narrowing her eyes, more curious about what Marcus didn't say than what he did. The morning breeze raced across her exposed flesh. She shivered, whether from cold or a sense of impending doom, she wasn't certain.

Avoiding Marcus's outstretched hand, she stepped around him, holding her wet skirts above her ankles. She would return to the castle. The next time she stood before Marcus he would remember what he'd been missing over the past months.

ROWENA ENTERED THE rear courtyard and was instantly set upon by both Gwendolyn and Fiona who had obviously been watching what happened below through the crenellations in the rear wall. Rowena was swept into the castle away from Marcus.

"We've been so worried." Fiona hooked her arm through Rowena's and conveyed her up the stairs towards the family bedchambers. Gwendolyn followed along more slowly with a hand below her swollen abdomen.

"Are you certain there is only one baby in there?" Rowena asked, concerned that at seven-and-a-half-months pregnant her sister-in-law seemed larger than most other expectant women she'd known.

Gwendolyn chuckled. "The last time Lottie checked, she only heard one heartbeat." The expectant mother rubbed a hand across her abdomen. "Don't worry. This little warrior simply wants to hurry this process along." She gained the top of the stairs then leaned against the banister to catch her breath. "Go on to the chamber. I'll catch up to you in a moment."

Fiona nodded and continued down the hallway with Rowena. "As soon as Mrs Morgan discovered it was you who came out of the water, she insisted on preparing a hip bath and a hot meal for you in your chamber."

The chatelaine had been like a second mother to all the MacLeod children. Entering the bedchamber, Mrs Morgan's kind eyes widened at the sight of Rowena. "Good heavens. Looks like you brought half of the kelp in the loch back in your hair." Before Rowena could say anything, her wet gown was loosened and lowered by the chatelaine while Fiona removed her half-boots and stockings. They both divested her of her undergarments until she stood naked before them.

"Get in the water," Mrs Morgan encouraged as she handed Fiona a thick shaving of heather-scented soap. "I'll leave you ladies to finish up here. Mrs Honey sent up a bowl of pottage and fresh bread from the kitchen."

Gwendolyn entered and sat on the bed, her feet dangling over the side while Fiona plucked kelp from Rowena's hair. "Marcus is back," Gwendolyn said with an arched brow.

"Marcus is back, but he's different than when he left." Rowena's stomach fluttered with nervousness. "He seems uncertain about us, about me." The happiness in his eyes had vanished.

"You have nothing to worry about," Fiona assured her, scrubbing her hair now with the soap. "He was so in love with you when he left. That kind of connection doesn't disappear no matter how long a couple has been separated."

"He's simply apprehensive, seeing you again," Gwendolyn said. "I was terrified to see Alastair after being separated for five years. But all the feelings we had for each other were still there. They simply needed to be coaxed out a bit. And that's where we come in." She winked at Fiona. "When we are done with you, he'll remember everything he gave up when he left."

At Gwendolyn's words of encouragement, the tiniest prick of hope sprang to life in Rowena's chest.

When her bath was finished, Gwendolyn held out a robe, then Fiona sat Rowena near the fire to dry her hair and encouraged her to eat. The simple meal tasted wonderful and warmed her in places the hot bath water had not.

Once she was through, Fiona got to work dressing her while Gwendolyn watched from the bed. A chemise with lace edging the low neckline was thrown over her head and stays were added then laced to push her breasts upwards. Stocking were rolled up over her legs and secured with a bow at her knees.

Rowena mustered a smile to match Gwendolyn and Fiona's excitement. There was so much emotion swirling inside her that she wasn't certain she wouldn't crumble once she stood before Marcus again, instead of remaining strong.

Fiona shook out a burgundy gown with little pink thistles stitched with silk thread along the hem and sleeves. Gathering it together, she tossed it over Rowena's head, allowing it to float down over her hips a moment before she cinched the back together. The full skirt belled out, making Rowena's waist look small. The stays lifted her breasts high so that the swell of them just breached the lace edge of the chemise above the gown's square neckline. And the pink thistles edging the hem and sleeves of her gown complemented the pink in her cheeks.

"You look lovely." Fiona stepped back and smiled.

Gwendolyn nodded her approval. "You're stunning."

"Now to see to your hair. Would you like a weaving? A plait?" Fiona asked as she picked up a brush.

"Leave it loose," Gwendolyn suggested. "Rowena looks perfect, except the dress needs one more thing." Gwendolyn stood and came towards Rowena holding out a small folded piece of linen. "A gift for you from your brother." Pulling back the edges of the linen, Gwendolyn revealed a strand of pink pearls. "These were your mother's. Alastair wanted you to have them."

Fiona took the necklace and fastened the pearls around Rowena's neck.

Despite her attempts to be strong and brave, tears burned at the back of her throat. "Thank you for your efforts. I hope they are enough to convince Marcus we belong together." She brought her fingertips up, running them over the pearls.

"The final touch," Fiona said, producing a pair of pink slippers.

Rowena held back the edge of the gown and worked her toes into the slippers. Her sisters-in-law had made her feel feminine and beautiful, but would it be enough to make Marcus desire her with the same intensity as he had not so long ago?

She drew a deep breath and headed for the door. There was only one way to find out.

CHAPTER SIX

A T THE TOP of the stairwell, Rowena drew a steadying breath before proceeding to the first floor and down a long hallway until she reached the doorway of the great hall. One glance inside the chamber revealed Marcus near the hearth. He had changed into a pair of dark breeches and a crisp white shirt, no doubt offered to him by one of her brothers. He moved with a restless grace; a deeper, powerful energy. At her entrance, he stopped and turned towards her, waiting for her to join him.

Now that the urgency of their previous reunion in the loch had faded and her emotions had settled, Rowena was able to see the true man before her. He had changed in the time they'd been apart. He had always been tall, at over six feet, but his physique was more mature now, his chest wider and deeper, his shoulders broader. The muscles of his thighs were heavier and clearly delineated by his attire. He must have endured heavy physical work during his time away.

She brought her gaze to Marcus's face. His eyes connected with hers and her body warmed. Some things about him had not changed at all. He was still handsome, and his gaze still had a slightly wicked appeal that was revealed in the soft candlelight. His long dark hair was neatly pulled back in a queue. Sideburns accented the high cheekbones of his slightly elongated face, his strong jaw, and deeply bronzed skin.

But it was his eyes that drew her in. Their green depths held her hostage as he waved her into one of two chairs set before the hearth. His eyes used to look at her with warmth and passion. There was nothing warm about him now. His gaze was cold and stark, almost haunted. "I'll admit I had imagined our reunion in a slightly different way than it played out this morning." He took the chair opposite hers.

Her fingers stretched towards him before she curled them against the arms of the chair, fighting herself. Once, he had swept her into a whole new world where nothing existed but their feelings for each other. Her surname hadn't mattered, and she'd clung to him, believing in hope and possibility. She'd been consumed by his brushfire passion and had been transformed by his devotion.

Rowena closed her eyes, mourning the loss of what they'd once had. If a spark of desire still remained, Marcus would have taken her in his arms by now. All of Fiona and Gwendolyn's efforts had gone to waste. He wasn't here to resume their interrupted hopes, he was here to say goodbye.

"Rowena?" Marcus's voice cut through her memories.

Rowena opened her eyes, shaking off the heaviness that had invaded her soul. Her gaze connected with his, her control once more in place. They sat staring at each other in awkward silence until Rowena said, "Your mother and father will be—"

"I saw them while you were dressing. They are pleased I have returned safely." Marcus's expression was tight, pained.

"Did you find what you were looking for on your quest?" Rowena asked, wanting to talk about anything but the two of them.

He nodded. "More than I ever could have hoped for, and yet it came with a terrible price."

Rowena frowned. "Then why did you not pay my ransom?"

"It's complicated." He stood, pacing before his chair like a caged animal. "My apologies," he said after a long silence and stopped before her. "I am not used to sitting, much less being inside. Would you care to go for a walk in the gardens?"

"We will be outside the castle walls." She got to her feet, maintaining her distance from him. "Are you worried that Bryce might return?"

His smile was the first honest emotion he'd shared since his return. It warmed the chill in his eyes. "I'll be there to protect you." He patted the broadsword at his side.

She crossed her arms in front of her but when she realised the action only pushed her already revealed bosom higher, she dropped her hands to her sides. "I am quite capable of taking care of myself."

"Then why did Bryce apprehend you?"

"He drugged me." She pressed her lips into a hard line as she headed for the door, needing to walk off some of her own pent-up tension.

Rowena stomped all the way down the stairs and out into the courtyard before her emotions settled. She wasn't really angry about Marcus thinking he could protect her better than she could herself. She was angry that he hadn't come for her immediately, for not paying her ransom, for not looking at her the way he used to. For changing everything.

She slowed her pace, allowing him to catch up with her until they stopped before the gates.

Aria stood guard. "Where are you two heading?"

"We needed to walk. The gardens seemed like the safest place," Rowena replied, expecting the portcullis to open.

Aria stepped before Marcus, staring him in the face. "Alastair asked me to monitor who comes and goes while he calls off the search for you." Her gaze narrowed on Marcus as her hand moved to the sword at her hip. "Besides, I do not know this man other than that he arrived along the shoreline this morning. Who are you and what are you doing with Rowena?"

Rowena turned to Marcus then back to Aria. "Forgive me. I forgot the two of you had not yet been introduced. Aria, this is Marcus MacDonald. A friend of our clan."

"A MacDonald?"

"He is the son of James and Agnes MacDonald. He's been at sea for the past six months and has only just returned."

Aria's features softened. "James and Agnes have been very kind to me since I arrived at Dunvegan."

Rowena stood there a moment feeling . . . guilty? Of what? Marcus was the one who had been absent as the rest of them moved on with their lives. She forced a congenial smile. "Marcus, this is our fairy sister, Aria. She came to us shortly before Orrick married Isolde."

"A fairy sister?" Marcus's brows shot up. "Orrick is married?"

"Aye." Rowena turned back to her new-found sister. "Aria is a welcome addition to our clan. She was vital to our success when the English invaded Dunvegan."

Marcus's pinched expression bespoke his confusion. "The English attacked you here?"

"Much has happened in your absence." Rowena glanced at the gates then back at Aria. "Please let us pass through to the gardens. We need to talk privately."

"You could talk in the library or the great hall. With so many of the men gone, everywhere in the castle is more quiet than usual."

"The gardens," Rowena said with a plea in her voice. She needed this time alone with Marcus if there was any chance of salvaging their relationship. "A shout would alarm you to any danger."

Aria's gaze narrowed while considering, then she released a tight breath. "If it is that important to you, then aye. Be on guard." She gave the order and the portcullis was raised, allowing Rowena and Marcus to pass through.

They crossed over the drawbridge and headed to the right before Marcus spoke again. "I must admit, hearing Orrick is married, the English attacked, you have a fairy relative, and that your clan is growing has me bewildered. For months I've been thinking that your life was static, that everything would be as it was when I left, and now I realise your life has changed every bit as much as mine has during our separation."

Rowena's heart raced when Marcus slipped his hand under her elbow, steadying her as they crossed over the bridge and the rocky path that led into the more formal gardens. Her sister-in-law, Fiona, had been hard at work sculpting the beds and adding native plants to fill in what had already been there. The effect was a riot of texture in variegated shades of green and a few springtime flowers. The wood anemone and snowdrops had come and gone, to be replaced with bluebells, blackthorn, and pussy willow.

As they came to the smoother path in the garden, Marcus drew his hand away, ending Rowena's momentary joy. "We've both changed over the months," Rowena agreed as she looked about the garden. There was a rebirth of life, both beauty in the variegated green and decay in the shrubs and dormant plants nature had reclaimed over the winter. 'Twas the cycle of life—from beauty to death and rebirth. Rowena's gaze shifted to Marcus. Is that what had happened to them? Had they lived through the beautiful part of their time together, and was she clinging to a dying relationship when she should simply let Marcus go? "Our friendship has come to an end."

"Never." Marcus frowned, keeping his gaze on the path before them. "I still care about you, Rowena, but my duties take me elsewhere. Many of my men died while searching for treasure. I owe support to their families to compensate for the loss of their loved one."

Rowena stopped walking and wrapped her arms about her waist, feeling that if she didn't, she would come apart. Marcus was saying goodbye, threatening to destroy the one steady relationship she'd ever had. With that goodbye, he would rob her of a future with a husband who would not leave her as everyone else in her life had. "I can understand your pain at the loss of your men, and it is admirable that you want to support their families, but locating each man's family could take you months, perhaps even years."

"Exactly." His features softened and his gaze lifted. For a heartbeat, he looked at her with eyes she remembered. "I will not make you wait for me to fulfil my duty. That is why I came here today—to release you from any commitment we made to each other."

"But we love each other." Rowena forced the words past the tightness in her throat. "Together we defied your clan and convinced my own that we belonged together. Or have you forgotten that?"

"Those two people no longer exist. Our time apart has changed us both. Me most of all."

"I do not believe that." Rowena's voice was fierce. "You and I had something special—something most people dream about but never achieve. How could six months and a little distance change a heart so much?"

Marcus pressed his lips together and looked away, but not before she saw a momentary flash of pain in his eyes. "I do not love you anymore, Rowena. How much more honest must I be? You must let me go for the benefit of us both."

The hot flash of anger that had overcome her faded, leaving in its place an emptiness the likes of which she'd never known before. "You would allow your sense of honour to destroy your own happiness?"

"I have no other option."

She could hear his own pain in the words. "You are a warm, caring, loving human being, Marcus. I have always valued that about you. I know you think it is noble and dutiful to care for your lost men, but when that is over, what will you have left with any meaning in your life if you turn your back on me?"

"Rowena—"

"I am willing to wait as long as it takes for you to complete your duty to your lost men."

"I don't want you to wait. I want you to live your life

without me." He looked at her and frowned. "I will not be returning to Dunvegan once I leave. Ever."

A terrible shudder swept through Rowena's body as she shifted her gaze from Marcus to the sky overhead. A crisp, salty breeze cooled her cheeks, matching the iciness settling inside her. Marcus was leaving her just as everyone else in her life had, but she wouldn't fall apart before him. Nay, she would save that for the privacy of her own chamber. She had dreamed of a life with Marcus every day for the past six months. Now he would rob her of everything with a simple goodbye. "There is nothing I can say or do to change your mind?"

"Nothing."

She'd learned long ago the futility of arguing with her brothers. Marcus appeared to be just like them once their mind was made up. To them, there was no other way forward except what they thought was right, no matter who was left behind or how much pain they endured. Rowena straightened. "Since there is nothing left to say, you should be going."

"Then we are agreed, it is best to part?"

Instead of confirming what he wanted to hear, she took a step away.

He caught her hand with his. "Rowena . . ."

A jolt of awareness tingled against her skin. She jerked her fingers away at the sensation. The effect of his touch on her senses was more pronounced than ever. She'd forgotten what it felt like, the physical manifestations of the soul-deep connection they'd once shared. Her body was still tuned to him, her nerves stretching when he drew near in telltale anticipation—an anticipation that could never be fulfilled. "I must go. Goodbye, Marcus."

Rowena turned away from the castle and ran down the path lined with trees that bordered the edge of the loch. She heard Marcus call after her but she dared not stop or go back. If he caught up with her, she would make a fool of herself and beg him to stay. He'd made his position clear. It was time for her to move forward with her own life—a life without Marcus.

Her heart hammered in her chest as her feet pounded on the gravel path, passing the walled garden entrance and on towards the birch trees. Mayhap she could lose him in the trees. She knew all the hiding spots in these woods, had used them during her youth to conceal herself when she and her brothers played hide-and-seek.

When she was into a small fringe of trees, she heard footsteps coming swiftly behind her. She took a deep breath to brace herself to confront Marcus—but it wasn't Marcus who came to a halt before her. It wasn't Marcus who grabbed her, and it wasn't Marcus who clamped a brutal hand over her mouth to stifle her scream.

CHAPTER SEVEN

"*R*OWENA!*"

Marcus cursed and chased after her. She had put an abrupt end to his practised speech. As much as it pained him, things were done between them. Though he would not leave her alone and unprotected outside the castle walls. Her brothers Alastair and Tormod would skin him alive if anything happened to her.

Marcus followed her down the path, keeping her in his sights until she broke from the path and headed into the birch trees. He was entirely to blame for her running away. He never should have reached for her hand, but the temptation to touch her one last time had overwhelmed him. Instant desire had flared as it always did. He'd looked into her hazel eyes and let the moment flow over him before she'd jerked her hand away. But the warmth had remained, paralysing him momentarily as he'd remembered everything he'd spent the last six months trying to forget.

"Rowena?" He stopped, listening for a reply, but there was only the flutter of bird wings overhead. An uneasy sensation pricked the nape of his neck. He stared hard into the trees on either side of him to determine if something was amiss, but he could see nothing. He could hear nothing but the breeze as it rustled the leaves overhead. Even so, his hand drifted to his sword as the uneasy feeling continued to grow.

He was about to turn around and head back to the path when, where there should have been only brown and green, he saw a bright patch of burgundy, and a red and green tartan.

The MacDonald colours.

Marcus surged forward, shouting alarm to the guards on the castle towers and to Aria and her men at the gates as he ploughed through the trees, following Rowena and her captor. He had to reach her before they made it to the loch.

The man dragging a very reluctant Rowena towards the shore and a boat waiting there must have sensed Marcus was closing in. The man stiffened. Like a fox catching the scent of fresh blood, he turned and Marcus saw who had abducted Rowena for a second time.

Bryce. A wave of anger, black and burning like acid, boiled up from the hidden depths of Marcus's soul. He pushed himself to his limits and erupted onto the shoreline just as Bryce plunged Rowena into the water, trying to force her into the waiting boat.

"Release Rowena." The words were squeezed through taut white lips. "This is between you and me. It always has been."

Bryce stopped then jerked Rowena against his chest. He

drew a dagger from his belt and held it at her throat. Even so, Rowena continued to kick Bryce in the shins. His features hardened at her continued assault. "She's the only leverage I have to make you do what I want. I will kidnap her as many times as it takes to force your cooperation."

Marcus took two steps towards the water but stopped when the dagger was pressed more firmly against Rowena's skin.

Rowena stopped struggling. Her hazel eyes held no fear, only anger.

Marcus's hand moved to the hilt of his sword. Behind him, the rapid footsteps of the castle guards grew ever closer. "You will soon be outnumbered."

"You are already in jeopardy," Rowena said, her gaze shifting to the left, towards the shoreline. "Release me this instant or Aria will put an arrow through your heart."

Marcus drew his sword and dropped into position even as his own gaze shifted to the shores of Loch Dunvegan. Aria raced towards them, an arrow nocked and ready to fire.

"Her aim is quite accurate," Rowena said. "Or would you rather test her abilities with your life?"

Bryce turned so that Rowena's body was between him and the female warrior. "Tell the woman to lower her bow and arrow."

Marcus took primitive delight in the sudden fear in his cousin's eyes. "Not until you release Rowena."

Bryce shoved Rowena forward as he took cover behind

the boat.

In a heartbeat, Marcus sheathed his sword then raced to catch Rowena before she tripped over the weight of her sodden gown. He helped her to shore before turning back to his cousin. With Rowena out of danger, Marcus drew his sword once more and plunged into the water after his cousin. "Get in that boat and leave this isle. Go find your own way in this life, Bryce. For you'll not get another chance to torment the MacLeods."

"You're no MacLeod, or have you forgotten?" Bryce snarled. "Besides, kidnapping Rowena again was simply a ruse to get the castle to let down its guard. By now, my men have captured your parents. Since you wouldn't turn over your portion of the treasure for Rowena, then perhaps you'll do so for the safe return of your parents."

Dredging up every fibre of strength and speed in his powerful legs, Marcus dropped his sword and launched himself into the water and drove a fist upwards into Bryce's jaw.

Bryce staggered back a step, his head whipped violently to one side by the blow. Marcus delivered a second blow, but Bryce lifted his left arm to block it and punched Marcus in the gut with his right, sending him staggering backwards.

It didn't take long for Marcus to recover as he lunged forward, the two cousins coming together like enraged bulls. Grunts and curses rent the air as they traded punches in the thigh-deep water. The smell of sweat and rage steamed the air between them.

Ten guards entered the water. It took three men to pull Bryce back to the shore and seven to keep Marcus from following.

Aria stood between them at the water's edge, her gaze fixed on Marcus. "Killing this man will not help us to free James and Agnes."

"I'd rather die than tell you where I've hidden them." Bryce strained against the men who were holding him as he spat out a bloodied chip of tooth along with an indecipherable curse.

"You would bring harm to your own aunt and uncle?" Marcus surged forward, dragging the guards with him.

"I'll kill them if I have to in order to get that treasure from you."

Marcus's chest heaved as he tried to suppress his anger. Beating his cousin to a pulp would not help his parents. "I will not give you that treasure until I make reparations to the families of the men who died bringing it to the surface."

"Then prepare to never see your parents again."

Marcus looked directly at his cousin. "I did not say there wasn't something I could offer you now."

Bryce's shoulders relaxed as the fight went out of him. "Go on."

"There is another treasure that still needs to be recovered. Though in order to obtain it, you must first release my parents, then come with me aboard *The Cliodna*."

Bryce's gaze narrowed. "What? So you can toss me overboard? Nay. You bring the treasure to me."

Marcus shook himself free from the men who still held him but did not advance on his cousin. "If you want this treasure, then for once in your life you are going to have to earn it."

Bryce wiped a trickle of blood leaking from his lip. "And where will you take me? To some foreign land where once the treasure is recovered, you will leave me behind?"

"The treasure is in Scotland. You will receive your cut just like everyone else aboard the ship and will be offered the same protections as any of my men."

Bryce pressed his lips into a thin line. "I am a MacDonald. Your cousin. I deserve better treatment than your men."

"You are a cheat and a scoundrel. This is the only offer I will ever extend. Take it or find yourself an unwilling guest in the MacLeods' dungeon for the rest of your life."

Bryce's gaze narrowed. "To make certain you protect me, I will not release your parents until after the treasure is found."

Marcus set his jaw uncompromisingly. "Nay. No parents, no treasure."

Bryce shot him a malevolent glare. "How do I know you aren't lying to me? Perhaps there is no treasure at all."

"We will find gold and silver ingots, coins, gemstones, jewellery, and wine, from what I was told."

Bryce's features brightened. "I'm still not certain I can

trust you."

"You have nothing to lose by doing so," Marcus replied, noting a shift in Bryce's stance. Had his cousin finally realised he had no other option?

Bryce heaved a heavy sigh. "Very well. I will return your parents to Dunvegan this evening. But if you are lying to me or betray me in any way, I will find a way to kill you."

"I'd like to see you try," Marcus replied as he walked back to the shoreline. "Return my parents unharmed, and we have an accord."

The tension amongst those gathered drained visibly as the two men clasped each other's shoulders then stepped apart. "Be forewarned, Bryce. The desolate cave we seek is shrouded in superstition and believed to be a portal to either Hell or the fairy realm. Many have tried to uncover the secrets held deep within the Cave of Gold never to be seen or heard from again."

"I'm already living in Hell as a fringe MacDonald, accepted by no one." Bryce shrugged. "I'll take my chances on a bunch of superstitious nonsense."

Marcus picked up then sheathed his sword, noting the glances of the MacLeod clansmen had shifted from tense to interested. "I'll not ask any of you to put yourselves in danger over my cousin's folly."

Mathe and Crayton, two of the men who had held him back from Bryce, stepped towards Marcus. "What if some of us want to come with you?" The two men's gazes passed over several of the others on the shore. Many nodded their agreement.

"Treasure hunting is a dangerous business. I am honoured by your request, but your duty is to Dunvegan and Laird MacLeod, first and foremost. But," Marcus added, drawing out the word, "when Alastair returns, and if he agrees, I could take ten of you with me as long as you understand the hazards you might face." He would have them fully aware of the risk to their lives before they ever set foot on his ship.

The men started talking excitedly amongst themselves as they and Aria headed back towards the castle. Bryce returned to his boat and rowed away. And finally, when he could avoid looking at her no longer, Marcus's glance lifted from the sodden hem of Rowena's gown to her trim waist and upwards to the creamy flesh of her bosom. Her chin tipped up and he allowed his gaze to lift to her lips. He wondered how her lips would taste now that they'd been apart for so long . . .

As if following his thoughts, she slowly stiffened, steel infusing her. He was jerked back to full awareness when her lips firmed. He glanced up at Rowena's eyes—and found them blazing. "You'll sacrifice your goals to save your parents, but spare nothing for me?"

He opened his mouth to tell her his parents had no one but him, but she silenced him with a daggered look.

"I am sick to death of the MacDonalds. First, I am kidnapped and held prisoner by your laird, Alexander MacDonald, and almost raped by your cousin, Bryce. Six months later, Bryce kidnaps and holds me hostage, and then a second time threatens my life with a blade to my throat. Then there is you . . . You claimed to love me, but now that you are a wealthy man, you cast me aside."

"I've explained my reasons."

Her gaze hardened. "If you truly loved me, you would have asked me to go with you while you assuage your guilt and offer settlements to the families of the men you lost."

He bristled at her implication that it was his own guilt that drove him, but a heartbeat later recognised her words as the truth. It was the guilt that he had survived their attempts to bring the treasure to the surface, when others had been dashed against the rocks, eaten by sharks, or drowned. So he offered the only other reason he had not asked her to travel with him. "Travel has become extremely dangerous with English patrols camped across the Highlands."

"More dangerous than being kidnapped in your own garden or along the shore of your home? There is danger everywhere. You need not pretend any longer that is the reason for your change of heart."

He couldn't argue with her logic. She'd experienced the harsh reality of the English occupying Scottish territory first-hand. Knowing he was outmatched, he asked, "What is it that you want, Rowena?"

"If you are going to take ten MacLeods with you on your

treasure hunt, then I want one of those MacLeods to be me."

He shook his head. "Alastair would never allow that."

"He would if you married me before we left."

His eyes widened at her suggestion. "Marry you? Why would you want to marry me? Only a moment ago you were railing against all the MacDonalds. Why would you want to become one yourself?"

"Our union will protect me from the men aboard your ship."

Perhaps, but who would protect her from him? "You are not coming with me." His words were firm.

She ignored his response. "Prove to me that not all MacDonalds are abominable humans. Besides, if we do not consummate the marriage, then we can have it annulled upon our return."

Not consummate the marriage while being confined to close quarters for weeks on end when the obvious attraction that had brought them together still existed between them? There had to be more to this mad idea of hers. "Why is it so important you come with me to locate the treasure?"

"Because I want a fair share of the treasure so I can create a future for myself, by myself."

He frowned. "Your family will never allow you to go off on your own."

She scowled at his quick response. "Aye, they will. Changes abound at Dunvegan. Orrick and Isolde are away at Dunshee Castle. Tormod and Fiona are rebuilding Ulster

Castle for a future home. Alastair and Gwendolyn are starting a family. No one needs me to be their spinster sister. And I am tired of everyone abandoning me. So I will start a life of my own where the only person who can disappoint me is me."

She would never leave her family. Would she? "What about Callum?"

"Callum is an adult now. He will find his own way eventually and have no need of me, just like the rest."

Marcus understood her pain at being left behind by those around her. He'd experienced the same thing amongst the MacDonalds. He'd wanted more out of his life than constant warring with the other Highland clans, especially the Mac-Leods, for no particular reason other than to disrupt the status quo. That was why he'd started sailing—to escape it all. First in a small dinghy he'd reclaimed from the sea, then larger boats that he'd rescued, repaired, and sold in order to finally purchase a sailing ship.

A ship of his own had been his only dream, until he'd met Rowena along the shores of Loch Dunvegan and had started to dream of other things. But those dreams had come to an end when tragedy had befallen his first treasure-hunting exploration. He'd convinced himself that making settlements on his lost crew members' families was more important than Rowena.

They'd never really talked about their goals and dreams with each other in the past. Reviewing his own dreams and hearing her articulate her own made him pause. He'd never realised how alone and isolated Rowena had been after the death of her parents and when her three oldest brothers left her to pursue their own lives away from Dunvegan. She had love, affection, and concern for her family, yet she wanted something of her own. The very idea made her seem more real to him than she ever had before.

Marcus stilled as another thought occurred to him. Like the sailors he'd lost, did he owe her something tangible to compensate for a life that no longer included marriage to him? A resigned sigh escaped him. "I would agree to sharing a portion of the Cave of Gold's treasure with you if you stay behind at Dunvegan."

"Nay," she replied in a tight voice. "I want more."

"How much more?"

"I want to go on an adventure for once in my life and be free of the constricting walls of Dunvegan."

He shook his head. "Alastair will never agree to that."

"He would have no say in the matter if we were married."

Marcus groaned. As a married woman, Rowena's husband would determine her fate. Though he doubted Rowena would follow anyone's guidance but her own. Married or not. That trait was initially what had drawn him to her. She hadn't cared about his surname or that her clan might have reservations about the two of them.

Sensing he was softening to the idea, Rowena's lips

quirked. "I promise to start the annulment proceeding the moment we return. You can get back to your duty to your fallen crewmen, and you'll never have to see me or my kinsmen again." The words rang with outright challenge.

Marcus's jaw tightened. How else could he dissuade her? He took a step closer, then another until his face was close to hers. His nerves flickered as the scent of heather teased his senses. "In order to receive an annulment, you must prove you are yet untouched. A physical inspection would be required."

Rowena didn't step back or react in any fearful way to his blatant intimidation. "I am up to the task, I assure you."

He studied her eyes. The sun overhead reflected in the hazel depths, making them appear gold one minute, shadowed green the next—mysterious, ever-changing, much like the sea. A lick of desire slid down his spine when he noted her breathing had quickened along with his own.

The air between them all but crackled. She met his gaze with a steely one of her own. "You will marry me then, and take me with you."

"You say that as though I had any other choice."

"You don't."

A pulsing throb beat at his temple as he looked over Rowena's shoulder towards Dunvegan. "A marriage in name only."

A smile played at the corners of her mouth, casting out the shadows that had taken refuge there in his absence.

"Agreed."

"Shall we head back to the castle and wait for my parents' return together?" He offered her his hand. She accepted and curled her fingers around his larger one. If taking her with him would provide her a future and clear his conscience, then that's what he would do, even though everything inside him screamed to find another solution.

By nightfall a MacDonald would be married to a MacLeod.

CHAPTER EIGHT

B RYCE KEPT HIS word and brought Marcus's parents back to Dunvegan by midday. Shortly after, Alastair, Tormod, Callum, Graeme, and their men returned. The castle teemed with people and excitement at the news that Rowena and Marcus would marry within the hour. Now that the moment was upon her, Rowena's thoughts had shifted from joyous to troubled. She was forcing the man she loved into a lie, manipulating him every bit as much as Bryce was doing.

Rowena sat on the edge of her bed, dressed in nothing but her shift and a dressing gown as she stared at the beautiful seafoam gown Gwendolyn had brought her. "I had it made just for this occasion when Marcus left so we would have it prepared upon his return."

Alastair had paid for the gown, so he must have supported the idea then, but he had seemed confused when Marcus had announced their intention to marry that afternoon. He'd asked her to go to her chamber and wait for him while he talked to Marcus.

A knock on the door startled Rowena from her thoughts.

"Come in," she said, bracing for the interrogation to come.

Alastair entered the chamber then shut the door behind him before pulling a chair closer to her bedside. "I need to make certain all is well here before I can give you my blessing." He glanced at the dress hanging on her armoire then back at her. "Only this morning Marcus told me he needed to break his promise to you in order to fulfil other obligations. What has changed in a matter of hours?" His gaze narrowed as though trying to read her thoughts.

Rowena couldn't clear her brow of a frown, born of frustration, that had settled there. "Marcus changed his mind after we saw each other again. I'm certain he told you that when you spoke with him."

A slow smile transformed Alastair's face. "He said he'd fabricated an image of the woman he'd left behind over the months he'd been gone, and that image did not stand up to the woman you truly are."

Rowena didn't know whether to be pleased or insulted by Marcus's words. "So you'll agree to our union?"

"If you tell me this is what you want, I will not stand in your way."

"'Tis what I want," Rowena said more sadly than she'd intended, as she realised how disappointed her brothers would be in her when she finally did reveal the truth. Alastair hadn't considered her feelings when he'd left her at Miss Doddie's School for Girls, or when she'd had to make her way back home alone so that Callum would have family near him. Why should it matter what her brother thought about her when the treasure hunting was done? It shouldn't, but it did.

Marcus had obviously appeased her eldest brother during his own interrogation. He'd lied to Alastair, telling her brother the things he wanted to hear despite the fact Rowena had trapped him in a cage of her own design. Her stomach knotted as she tried to imagine how she and Marcus would move forward once they were wed. He would have to stand up to Alastair once again as he took her with him to find the treasure Bryce demanded. But how would her new husband treat her as they lived amongst his men? Would he resent her? Punish her?

She knew Marcus to be honourable and just. He'd proven that when he'd left his own clan to help the MacLeods. But he was also in the habit of command now, and determined to have things his own way, as he'd proven while standing up to Bryce. There was no real way to know for certain how he would react to their forced nuptials until they set sail.

Blind to the turmoil inside her, Alastair stood and leaned forward to kiss her cheek. "You'd best get ready for your wedding. Gwendolyn and Fiona are at the door, waiting to help you prepare."

The moment Alastair left, Gwendolyn and Fiona entered Rowena's bedchamber. In a flurry of activity, the two women arranged her hair, weaving a string of pearls through the long, dark locks, then dressed her in the lovely green gown. They finished the preparations of the bride in a joyous discussion of the wedding to come, and before Rowena knew it, they were heading down the hallway to the stairs that would take her to Marcus.

At the top of the stairs, Mrs Morgan, the chatelaine, placed a bouquet of Scots bluebells in shades of lilac and periwinkle blue in Rowena's hands. "Thank you, Mrs Morgan," Rowena said with a smile of gratitude, for the woman had been a part of her life since infancy. "I hadn't considered flowers, or anything else for that matter."

Mrs Morgan patted Rowena's arm. "Mrs Honey and I have everything ready. Your wedding might have been short notice, but we have not forgotten a thing."

"I am grateful," she replied before Gwendolyn and Fiona whisked her down the stairs. The wedding party waited at the doorway of the chapel. Alastair and Tormod smiled when they saw her, but Marcus stared at her, the expression on his face a mixture of appreciation and irritation.

Marcus's hair was tied back in a black riband that made him look like a pirate, but his clothing was something only a gentleman of means would wear. He was dressed in black breeches, a black waistcoat and coat trimmed with gold lace, with a snowy-white shirt with lace sleeves and jabot. His parents flanked him, as if he were a man headed off to battle. James and Agnes's expressions were severe, making Rowena wonder if they had suffered at the hands of their nephew, or if Marcus had told them the truth about why he was marrying Rowena in such haste.

The marriage contracts were laid out on a small table beside the chapel doorway. Marcus had already signed them, so Rowena picked up the quill and added her signature. Once that task was complete, Marcus and his parents headed inside the chapel.

Rowena's throat ached from the tension within her as she watched them go. The others who had been milling about followed, until she stood with only her older brothers beside her. She had expected to be filled with joyous excitement on her wedding day, not weighed down with guilt. Forcing her emotions aside, Rowena pasted a serene smile on her lips as Alastair and Tormod walked her into the chapel. At Marcus's side, Alastair and Tormod pressed a kiss to her cheeks before moving to join their wives in the small chamber.

Midday light streamed through the stained glass window, bathing the altar in a golden glow. As she approached, she shivered despite the warmth in the chamber. Marcus must have noticed because he reached for her hand. Warmth flowed from his strong grasp into hers as he gazed at her, taking in the pearls in her hair, at her ears and throat, and the small freshwater pearls dotting the surface of her gown.

His lips twitched. "The vision of you this morning in the loch is quite at odds with the woman before me now. Though both women were borne of the sea."

Heat rose to her cheeks. "Gwendolyn knows I am fond

of pearls."

He acted like a man who was well pleased with his bride despite the fiction of this marriage arrangement. She suspected that even the sharp-eyed Reverend Vollar could detect no inconsistency in Marcus's manner towards his bride.

The reverend cleared his throat, signalling his desire to begin. "Who gives this woman into a husband's keeping?"

"Her brother and I," Alastair responded in a clear voice.

The old reverend's gaze travelled over those assembled behind Rowena and Marcus. "And is there anyone to object—any impediment to this marriage?" There was a chorus of 'nays' before the minister turned back to the couple before him. "Then we shall proceed."

Rowena swallowed thickly, fighting the knowledge that her marriage would be based on a lie. In the days ahead, she would have to find some way to atone for her sin.

At a nod from the reverend, Marcus changed hands, taking her right hand in his and setting her bouquet on the altar.

"Do you, Marcus MacDonald, take this woman for your wife, to have her, to hold her, to honour her, so long as you both shall live?"

"I do," Marcus said in a clear, loud tone that held no trace of anger as she'd expected.

"And you, Rowena MacLeod, do you take this man for your husband, promising to obey him in all things, to be true and faithful to him, to honour him, so long as you both shall live?"

Panic rose up, threatening to choke her with the finality of what she was about to do. Unable to respond verbally, she nodded.

Reverend Vollar looked up, frowning. "I'd hear you speak the words."

She swallowed roughly, keeping her eyes fastened on the hand that held hers, and said, "I do."

"Then may God, who is just and merciful, from whom all things come, bless this union between you and make you fruitful, that you may bring forth sons and daughters to praise his name."

"So be it," Marcus said.

"So be it," Rowena echoed, cringing at yet another lie she would have to make amends for when their marriage was dissolved.

"Do you have a ring for your bride?" the reverend asked.

Rowena shook her head, but Marcus released her hand and retrieved a ring with a single emerald at the centre from his waistcoat. As he gently eased the ring onto her finger, she suddenly recognised it as her mother's ring. She shifted her gaze to Alastair, who smiled back at her and then to her mother hovering at the back of the chapel. Her mother's ghostly eyes shone with pride as she nodded.

Tears formed in Rowena's eyes, but she forced them back. She would have to return the ring to Alastair when this fabrication was over, but for now she would enjoy having the ring as a connection to the woman her mother was before becoming a ghost, to see Rowena through the days ahead.

Marcus took both her hands in his as the reverend announced, "As Marcus and Rowena have pledged themselves before God and witnesses, they are henceforward man and wife." To Marcus he said, "You may kiss your bride."

Marcus pulled her close and set his lips to hers. This kiss was just for show, Rowena assured herself. Even so, Marcus's nearness buffeted her senses, ripping her from reality. His lips were hard and demanding, searching for a response she longed to give, but knew she should not. He tilted his head, his lips moving over hers in a powerful, elemental call to her senses. Fragment by fragment, she lost her will to resist and when he parted his lips, she slid her tongue between and tasted what she had been denied for the past six months.

Passion.

It burst upon her, upon her senses, in a hot flood tide. It rose from within him, from between them, cascade upon cascade of exquisite sensation before he pulled back, leaving her breathless.

Cheers rose up from those gathered but the sound could not drown out the frantic beat of her heart in her ears. She might have forced him into this marriage, but with one kiss Marcus had demonstrated he had power over her in a way that defied logic and reason. Rowena swallowed roughly and looked into Marcus's eyes. Confusion that matched her own stared back at her. That more than anything helped her senses settle as she and Marcus turned towards those who were gathered. The hard part was behind her. All she had to do now was to make certain he never kissed her again, and everything would be fine.

A supper banquet followed the ceremony in the great hall. Seated beside Marcus, Rowena allowed herself to relax for the first time since the wedding had begun. Mrs Honey had managed to prepare an impressive spread given the short notice she'd had. As they waited for each course to be served, the discussion at table turned from congratulations to questions about what the couple would do now.

"As a gift for your wedding, Gwendolyn and I would like to offer you the newly refurbished north wing of the castle as your own living quarters," Alastair offered.

"I don't know what to say . . ." Rowena replied to the very generous offer.

"Rowena can stay with us and remodel the north wing however she likes until you can rejoin her after you and Bryce settle this matter between the two of you," Alastair continued.

Marcus scanned the faces of those gathered before arching an eyebrow warily. "Rowena is coming with me. We are leaving for *The Cliodna* before sunset."

All conversation at the head table ceased. "You can't be serious." Alastair gaped at Marcus as if he could not possibly have heard correctly.

Marcus returned Alastair's gaze. Only the squared ridge

of his jaw betrayed the control it was taking to keep his emotions in check. "The only change to my plans is that they now include your sister."

Alastair's face tightened. "You would endanger my sister's life?"

"I mean to protect my wife at all costs."

"Alastair," Gwendolyn's calm voice intruded as she placed a hand on her husband's arm. "Your sister is now Marcus's wife. You must let her have her own life."

The muscles in Alastair's jaw worked furiously. "She's not prepared for life at sea."

Rowena opened her mouth to object, but a look from Gwendolyn stopped her. "Your sister has been raised to be as resilient as any of her brothers. It's time to let her have the freedom she longs for and allow Rowena and Marcus to start their married life together. Would you have wanted to be parted on our wedding night for weeks or even months?"

"Nay," Alastair agreed. "But—"

Gwendolyn shook her head. "There is nothing left to say except to wish them well and to have a safe journey." There was no threat to her words. They were a statement of fact.

"When did you become so wise?" Alastair smiled at his wife, nodding his acceptance. "It appears my wife has become your champion, Rowena."

"Nay," Rowena replied as she watched the tension ease from Marcus's muscles. "She simply knows what battles to fight and which to let go. An ability that will serve her well amongst the MacLeod men."

Everyone at the table laughed except Marcus, who had little to say over the next hour as the meal progressed from Cullen skink; haggis, neeps, and tatties with whisky sauce; beef filet, scallops, and vegetable terrine with plum sauce; plenty of claret; and clootie dumplings for dessert.

As the evening wore on the gaiety increased now that the uncomfortable discussion of Rowena leaving had been accomplished. When rays of evening sunshine filtered in through the windows in the great hall, Marcus pushed his chair back and stood, offering Rowena his hand. The earlier tension returned to Rowena's stomach as she slipped her hand in his.

"It's time," Marcus said, signalling that she should say her goodbyes.

After several embraces, a few tears, and many well-wishes, Marcus led her from Dunvegan to the front court-yard where a mounted Bryce and two other horses waited. A coachman and three stable boys would follow them to *The Cliodna*. The coach held Rowena's trunk and a few supplies. The men from Dunvegan would return the carriage and horses to the castle after the voyagers set sail. The other nine men who had volunteered to help them on this voyage had eaten quickly then had taken Bryce's boat and one other over to where Marcus's ship waited.

Red and orange coloured the sky as they mounted. Rowena was grateful that they would ride to the ship. A wild romp across the moors was just what she needed to dispel her nervousness. The knots in her stomach would disappear once they were racing over the rugged terrain between Dunvegan and Neist Point.

The others had followed them outside, but only Alastair and Gwendolyn approached them. Alastair reached up to squeeze Rowena's hand before turning to Marcus. "Take care of her."

Marcus smiled. "I will." The words sounded every bit as binding a vow as the ones he'd made to her earlier this day. He nudged his horse towards the gate, with Rowena at his side. Bryce followed behind.

The horses needed no urging when the reins were loosened, giving the horses the freedom to set their own pace as they made the eight-mile journey. Neither Marcus nor Bryce felt a need to converse, which suited Rowena. Instead, she gloried in the rush of the wind on her face as she listened to the clomping of the hooves on the rocky terrain. Only once did she glance at Marcus, then looked ahead, smiling. He seemed so much more at ease now that they were both free of her family and the walls of the castle. By the time they reached the shoreline on the opposite side of the peninsula, the sun was a fiery orb, slowly disappearing into the waters below.

Marcus and Bryce dismounted, then Marcus helped her down while Bryce returned the horses to the carriage that had rumbled to a stop shortly after they arrived.

At the edge of the cliff overlooking the sea, Rowena drew in a breath of tangy air and glanced at the double-masted brigantine anchored just offshore. From this distance, the ship looked small, at least smaller than she remembered. With her next breath, the reality of her situation crashed down around her. This ship would be her home for the next few weeks, perhaps even months. She and Marcus would be in close quarters, sleeping in the same small bedchamber. Close. Too close.

"Rowena?" Marcus spoke from behind her.

She turned towards him, and desire lanced painfully through her.

His gaze narrowed on the flush that rose to her cheeks. "Have you had a change of heart?" he asked with a hint of amusement in his voice. He pulled her into his arms.

Her heart in her throat, Rowena willed herself to relax. The warm scent of his skin filled her senses, overriding the fragrance of the sea. She steeled herself against the allure of his presence. She couldn't surrender to her emotions. They hadn't even made it onto the ship yet. Straightening her spine, she dug deep inside for the necessary determination to survive this adventure without surrendering herself to him. "I have not changed my mind. It's just that—I hadn't considered how intimate we will be during this voyage."

Marcus's arms tightened around her possessively, protectively. "In order to keep up appearances, we will have to sleep in the same bed, dress in the same chamber. We will be man and wife in all ways but one."

She stepped out of his embrace. With her head held high, but shaken to her toes, she headed for the path that led to the shoreline and the boat that waited there. Everything was happening so fast. Rowena's thoughts were in a turmoil as she navigated the path down to the shore. Over the last six months she'd wanted nothing more than freedom from her overprotective family. Now that she had her independence, at least temporarily, because of her marriage to Marcus, she had no idea what came next.

Once they found the treasure, she would have to uphold her end of their bargain and seek an annulment, setting Marcus free to settle his debt to his men. Would she be forced to return to her family? Or could she use her own newfound wealth to secure a small home for herself in a village somewhere on the isle and live there in isolation for what remained of her days?

Rowena reached the beach and paused, watching the orange-crusted sun set over the shimmering water, its rays stretching seemingly for miles. That future sounded as bleak and lonely as her past had been.

Marcus joined her on the beach and she turned to him, watching as the sea breeze ruffled his hair. "Are you ready to go aboard?"

"Aye. I'm ready," she said as she followed him to the waiting boat that would take them to *The Cliodna*. The real problem was that she didn't want to be free of Marcus. Yet she wouldn't trap him in a marriage he didn't want either, no matter how much passion shimmered in her blood every time they touched.

She had learned to do difficult things all her life. She could find the strength necessary to coexist with her new husband without exposing her true emotions to him. Hadn't she done that with her own family for years?

The days ahead would give Rowena time to determine the best way to move forward once, or even if, they found the treasure hidden deep within the Cave of Gold. If found, the gold there could buy her many things, but not the one thing she truly wanted: Marcus's love.

CHAPTER NINE

ROWENA STOOD AT the railing watching the shoreline as the sixteen-gun brigantine, *The Cliodna*, drifted out towards deeper waters. The ragged cliffs of the Isle of Skye were stark and dramatic, filling her with breathless wonder. Seals speckled the shoreline, almost imperceptible except by their barks that were caught and stolen by the wind. Overhead, the sharp cries of gulls came keening on the currents high above. Farther down the coastline, she identified Dunvegan Castle, which stood in stark golden contrast against a backdrop of indistinguishable greens and browns. She tried to commit the shoreline to memory, as if the remembrance was a talisman she could take on the adventure ahead.

Turning away from what would, pray God, not be her last glimpse of home, she noted that Bryce stood farther down the railing. His features were pinched as he gazed at the water, then back at the men. Marcus had not immediately asked him to help. Most likely because he had no experience as a sailor.

Ignoring Bryce, Rowena clutched the wooden barrier

tightly as nostalgia coiled in her chest. She was leaving the only home she'd ever known for an unknown adventure—an adventure that would challenge her both physically and mentally. She did not fear death, even though many of Marcus's men had died while searching for a previous treasure. For she had brought with her something they did not have: Fiona's fairy armour. The leather garments had protected her sister-in-law from the English. Rowena prayed they would keep her safe as she searched for the treasure of *Uamh Oir*. For only once this new treasure was found would Bryce leave them all in peace.

She searched the ship's deck for Marcus. He stood at the helm, shouting orders to his crew. Men—dressed in blue and white striped shirts with red handkerchiefs tied loosely about their necks—hurried across the deck in response to his commands, unfurling sails and tightening ropes. The ship picked up speed as the white canvas caught the wind, propelling them forward, the Scottish shoreline gradually receding in the fading light of the day.

Rowena marvelled at the flurry of activity before her, and her thoughts turned to Marcus. Their journey had begun. There was no turning back. Marcus had married her so that she could follow him aboard his ship, but she did not do so blindly. Her reaction to him earlier was simply a warning, preparing her for the challenges that lay ahead. She lifted her chin. The wind tugged at the loose ends of her hair. A need to feel the breeze more fully came over her. Rowena reached up and plucked the strand of pearls from her hair, then removed the pins until her dark brown locks flowed about her shoulders, only to be caught and lifted by the nautical wind.

A surge of pure satisfaction came over her as she closed her eyes and leaned into the sensations. Freedom was hers at last.

"Are you ready to go to the captain's quarters?" Marcus asked from behind her.

After a final look at the shoreline, Rowena tore her gaze away. "Aye," she said, following him to the stern until they reached an ornately carved door with a scene of a beautiful woman with long, flowing hair standing on a rock, surrounded by the sea. Over her head flew a seabird with rays of light emanating from both. On shore in the distance was an apple tree with three birds perched amongst the branches. "Does the carving have any significance?"

Marcus nodded, pointing to the woman. "This is the Otherworld goddess Cliodna in her earthly form. She is the goddess of the sea, the Otherworld, passion and love, and beauty. In Celtic lore she is the daughter of the Sea God, Manannán, who rules over the Isles. Every ninth wave is sacred to her. If you whisper a wish between the two halves of a shell, tie it with seaweed, then cast it onto a ninth wave that reaches the shore, she will grant your wish." He lifted his finger to the bird. "It is also said that Cliodna is followed by three brightly coloured birds who eat apples from a mystical tree in the Otherworld, and whose sweet songs heal the sick." He turned back to Rowena. "This ship is named for her so that her spirit will provide safe passage to those who travel aboard." His features shuttered as his hand dropped to his side. "That has not always been my experience to date."

He was remembering the men he'd lost. She frowned. "Their deaths were not your fault. Not even some mystical goddess could have saved them from a merciless sea."

"They were under my command." Marcus's voice was clipped. "Therefore, their welfare falls on my shoulders." He turned back to the door and opened it. "The captain's quarters."

Before she could step inside, he offered her a bow. "I must return to my duty until we are fully underway. I will be back shortly. If you need me, ask one of the men."

Rowena watched him leave. Part of her wished he had stayed; the other half was glad he was gone. With a soft sigh of resignation, she stepped inside the extravagantly carved chamber. Five rectangular windows were opposite the door, with two others along the sides, bathing the room in the reddish-gold tones of sunset. A canopy bed with a burgundy and gold privacy curtain was on her right. Beyond the bed, tucked beneath the side windows was a privy. On the left were a dressing table, shelves, cabinets, and a desk with an hourglass, quills, ink, and paper to record the events of the voyage. Towards the door, black cannons stood as sentinels on either side of the chamber. Hanging on the walls above the cannons were a variety of swords, knives, and pistols; a stark reminder that this was a fighting vessel. In the centre of the chamber was a table with two chairs. Fine linens protected the table from the two gold candelabras, a golden bowl, and a filigreed chest that lay upon it. The floor was covered in finely woven gold and burgundy carpets. She wasn't certain what she'd expected, but it wasn't this beautifully decorated and opulent room.

A shuffle sounded at the door. She turned, half expecting to see Marcus only to find Bryce propped against the doorjamb, scowling at her. "My cousin will be living in the height of luxury while I will sleep in a hammock below with the rest of his men."

Rowena chose her words carefully. "Not only does Marcus own this ship, he also taught himself to sail. He has earned the right to every good thing that has come his way. Whereas you only seek to steal what you want, never having toiled a day in your life from what Marcus has told me."

Bryce's gaze hardened. "You know nothing about me or what I've suffered."

She surveyed him boldly. "Nay, I do not. I am sorry if you feel you have suffered, but most of your suffering, I am certain, comes as a result of your own choices. Be careful, Bryce. If you continue to act foolishly, you will either end up in gaol or dead."

A sudden stiffness infused his frame. "Is that a threat?"

Rowena's gaze shifted to the swords on the wall beside her. Two more steps and she could grab one if needed, but then so could Bryce. "I apologise if I offended you with the truth. This voyage will give you a chance to learn something about sailing and perhaps about who you are deep inside, if you open yourself to the possibility."

His scowl deepened. "Why would I take advice from a MacLeod? It is you who should watch your back. I'd hate for you to take ill, or worse yet, fall overboard."

At the undisguised intimidation, Rowena met Bryce's gaze. The two stared at each other in silent battle until she replied, "I am a MacDonald now, or have you forgotten? And if anything happens to me, I doubt you will ever see so much as a gold coin in your future."

Just then, a tall, wide-chested young sailor appeared with her trunk in his hands, forcing Bryce to step outside the captain's quarters for him to pass inside. The young man smiled at Rowena as he deposited the trunk near the door. "Milady, is there anythin' else ye need?"

"Nay," she replied with a warm smile of appreciation. "Thank you for bringing me my trunk. I wanted to change into something more suitable for open water."

"Yer fine as ye are. Ye look like a mermaid." He winked at her before turning to Bryce. His amusement vanished. "The captain asked ye tae come with me. He wants ye tae work with the rest of us."

"He does, does he?" Bryce growled, as he headed for the

door. "We'll see about that."

With a roll of his eyes, the sailor closed the door behind himself as he left. Rowena leaned back against the door and let the motion of the wooden ship soothe her rattled nerves. Bryce would not make this trip an easy one, but she was certain Marcus knew how to keep his cousin in check. At least she hoped so for all their sakes.

Finally, she pushed away from the door and went to stand before one of the rectangular windows, gazing out as twilight descended over the water. In the sky above, the moon hung low, and the first glimmer of stars penetrated the greyness that would soon be black.

In the quiet, she could hear her own breathing. Everyone who was familiar to her and everything she loved was far away by now. A droplet of water from the spray of the wake trickled down the windowpane. She reached out and traced its descent with her finger. In that moment she'd never felt so alone, but she'd also never felt so free.

HOURS LATER, THE ship was well underway to their destination and yet Marcus remained on deck. He drew a deep breath as he took the ship into deeper waters, grimly wondering if he'd made the right decisions to bring not only Rowena but Bryce aboard as well. Bryce, he knew from their past, would never stop until he got what he wanted.

Marcus had never understood that kind of self-destructive drive before, yet in this moment he did. Since he'd seen Rowena in her seafoam-green dress, hugging her every curve and studded with pearls, looking very much like the sea goddess for which his ship was named, he wanted her in a more physical way than he ever had before.

As her husband, she was his for the taking, yet he couldn't pursue a more intimate relationship with her. His need to appease his cousin, then take care of his men came first. Footsteps on the forecastle brought Marcus back to the moment.

"You married the girl." There was no accusation in Eck's voice, only curiosity. "Then on your wedding night, you leave her in your chamber by herself."

Marcus's hands tightened on the ship's tiller. "She is safer there, alone."

"Safe from you?"

At the query, Marcus's gut clenched. "Take the till," he said to the seaman standing behind him. He moved to the rail, gazing blindly out at the windswept sea. "I shouldn't have brought her, but she goaded me into it."

"And marrying her?" Eck asked, joining him at the rail.

Marcus frowned. "Was the only way to keep her safe—aboard this vessel."

"From whom? You? The other men?"

"It's hard to explain." Marcus recalled that moment on the shore of Loch Dunvegan when he'd realised how much he'd hurt Rowena by leaving. She'd looked so forlorn, bereft of purpose—broken. He'd done that to her when he'd left her behind to go find his fortune. It wasn't her fault that along with great gains had come misfortune. He'd thought he could abandon her and do what needed to be done, but one look at her gut-wrenching sadness had changed his mind.

Those same angry and lost feelings echoed inside him. He'd wanted nothing more than to take Rowena in his arms and hold her until the people they used to be returned, but he could not change the events of the last six months. Because of them, he had a moral obligation to his fallen men that must be fulfilled. Only when he'd executed his responsibilities as captain of his vessel would he be free once again to live his own life, albeit changed by the past.

Yet, looking at a heartbroken Rowena, he'd found it impossible to walk away from her again, at least in the short term, until he could determine how to give her the freedom she desired without him at her side. He'd agreed to marry her despite the fact it was a dangerous commitment to make, for he still loved her. The difficult task ahead would be not acting upon those feelings. His commitment to his men outweighed his own desires. At his long silence, Eck shrugged. "You need not explain yourself to me. We've been through far too much together."

Marcus pulled his gaze away from the inky water and turned to his first mate, his friend. "Rowena needs protecting while she is on this ship."

"I presume you want me to keep an eye on her when you cannot?"

"Aye." Marcus released his grip on the rail with a sigh. "It's long past time that I return to the cabin to see Rowena."

"She's probably asleep. It is the middle of the night, or have you forgotten?"

"Then I'll wait until she wakes up." His hunger to see her overrode the reason he'd been trying to maintain. He had to make certain she no longer looked as broken and forlorn as she had on the shore. They were too far into this journey to turn the ship around, but he didn't want her to suffer while she was away from her home either.

Marcus strode down the steps of the quarterdeck and approached his quarters. A moment later he stood beside his bed with a single candle in his hand, looking down at a sleeping Rowena's pale face. She'd changed into her night rail and in the pale gold light, she looked as delicate as the most fragile blossom. What had he been thinking to bring her aboard with him? The men he'd lost had been hale and hearty. What chance did Rowena have of standing up to the challenges of the sea?

Rowena's lids twitched as if she had suddenly become aware of someone watching her. She opened her eyes abruptly, her gaze totally alert and without fear.

Marcus's muscles locked with tension as her gaze fastened on his face. She stared at him without speaking, and

Marcus suddenly found himself uneasy. He reached out awkwardly and touched her cheek. "I'm sorry to wake you. I wanted to make certain you were well. I left you abruptly before. I apologise for that."

She didn't answer.

His hand dropped away from her face to rest at his side. "Is there anything you need?"

"I need something to do on this ship. You are putting Bryce to work. How can I contribute as well?"

"Every task on this ship is far too strenuous for you. Besides, you are my wife."

"In name only." She set her chin. "Do other wives sail with their husbands? And if so, what do they do all day besides sit in the cabin reading?"

"Very few women live their lives at sea, but those who do serve meals, clean quarters, or keep financial and inventory records. Things that I am certain you have never done in your life."

Her gaze narrowed. "Then that just proves how little you know of me, for I am quite capable of accomplishing all those things. I will begin with tidying up your cabin on the morrow. Once that is done, you can decide whether I start with the financial records or the inventory. I am quite good with numbers, besting my two older brothers many times during our classroom days. Orrick was another story. He excelled at anything academic."

Marcus set his jaw. An inventory of his portion of the

treasure would be helpful so he could divide things evenly between the families of the two-and-thirty men he'd lost. He shrugged, not wanting to appear too enthusiastic about her offer. It shouldn't surprise him that she'd been raised with the same education as her brothers. The MacLeods seemed quite progressive where women were concerned. "So be it. Having you involved in the daily routine of the ship might help perpetuate the ruse of our wedded bliss."

Rowena blushed. "We've been married one day. I doubt anyone expects such from us anytime soon."

"This should be our wedding night." Marcus flushed with annoyance as he deliberately let his gaze wander over her upper body that was not hidden beneath the coverlet. His gaze lingered on her breasts beneath the delicate linen of her night rail. Had there been more light, he was certain he would see the pink tips he remembered so well from past explorations.

"Fear not. I have no expectations of you, and I certainly can control my reaction to you."

With her challenge, Marcus's temper ignited, and all thought of keeping his distance fled. She could control her reaction to him, could she? He took a step towards her until he towered over the bed.

Her eyes went wide as she shuffled backwards, tangling herself in the covers as she did. Instead of putting distance between them, she had trapped herself in the centre of the bed.

He smiled at her predicament as he recalled that he'd always found her high spirits more than a little exciting. She had always been a challenge, and that heated his blood now as it had in the past.

Her eyes grew brighter as though expecting him to crawl into bed beside her. He knew that would be a mistake, but the need to touch her was great, so he reached for her hand, intending to pull it towards him so he could press a kiss to her palm.

Rowena chose that same moment to shift backwards. As he clasped her hand, she pulled him off balance and towards her body. She wrenched her hand away in order to free it. Too late. His knee hit the edge of the bed and he fell not next to her as he tried to manoeuvre while falling, but directly on top of her, pinning her beneath him.

Rowena shrieked, then continued to struggle beneath him.

Fearing he might be crushing her with his weight, he grabbed her by the hips and rolled so that his back lay against the mattress, forcing her to straddle him.

She had the ability to leave the bed any time she wanted, and yet she stayed atop him. Her chest rose and fell beneath the delicate fabric of her nightclothes. The temptation to raise his hands to cover her sweet mounds, exploring at his leisure, grew stronger by the second.

Marcus fisted his hands, trying to regain control of the aching need that flared inside him. He forced his gaze to her face and his breathing suspended. The same desire that heated his blood reflected in the dark depths of her eyes.

Marcus swore beneath his breath and reached for her hips again. He lifted her off his body, setting her down gently before he shifted off the bed. He stayed beside her, still overly aware of the heat of Rowena's body and the scent of heather on her skin.

"That was unfortunate," she said, with a hint of disappointment.

Marcus fisted his hands once more, desperately trying to keep them to himself when all he wanted was to reach for her and pull her against him once more. "It won't happen again." He took a step back, then another until he stood beside the chest of drawers that held his clothing and extra bedding. He withdrew a pillow and a wool blanket, settling them on the hard floor in front of the door. "I'll sleep here. You keep the bed."

"These are your quarters. Should I sleep—"

"No wife of mine will sleep on the floor." He settled onto the blanket and turned away from her. "Blow out the candle and get some sleep. You've got a busy day tomorrow taking inventory of my portion of the treasure from Sandwood Bay."

Moments later, she extinguished the candle, pitching the chamber in darkness. Even then, he could still recall the feel of her body pressing against his. With an inward groan, Marcus settled more deeply into his pillow. He doubted he would find any reprieve in sleep tonight or any night while Rowena remained on his ship.

CHAPTER TEN

ROWENA WOKE AFTER a troubled night of broken sleep and rolled to her side, glancing at the door. Marcus was gone. His pillow and blanket were neatly folded and set on the table in the centre of the chamber. Disappointment flared before she caught the emotion and forced it deep inside. Marcus had work to do on this vessel. And now, thanks to her persistence last night, so did she.

At the memory of the feel of Marcus's hard body beneath her own, her cheeks warmed. When he'd held her against the bed with his hands, warm shivers had radiated through every nerve. The hard contours of his body upon her own had seemed to merge with her softer ones in ways she hadn't expected. Heat had radiated from the juncture of her thighs, matching the heat radiating from him. She'd had the strangest urge to raise her hips and match heat to heat, but a fearful uncertainty had kept her from moving.

She and Marcus had shared many breathless kisses in the past, embraces and explorative touches, but nothing like what had occurred on the bed in this cabin. Rowena threw her legs over the side of the bed and sat up, listening to the sound of the wind and rain as it hit the sails. She'd lay abed long enough. It was time to earn her keep.

It took her a few moments to steady herself against the rolling of the ship, but once she rediscovered her equilibrium she quickly dressed in a simple rust-coloured gown with white pintuck lace at the sleeves and bodice. Grabbing a shawl, she left the chamber.

The rain had stopped. Between the wind and the swaying of the ship Rowena had difficulty making the short trip to the quarterdeck. Wind whipped the tendrils of her hair about her face and tugged viciously at her long skirts as she peered out across the lower deck, searching for Marcus.

The ship rose and fell with the waves. Each downward motion brought a new surge of tangy sea spray over the bow of the ship. The overpowering scent of salt assailed her nostrils. Sea mist stung her cheeks, forcing Rowena to shield her face as the ship crested each new wave stirred up by the storm. An errant cord whipped against the masts as wave after wave slammed the deck. The ship creaked and groaned under the assault but kept trudging on towards the endless horizon and into the morning light.

With the sound of the waves echoing in her ears, she mused at how, along with this ship, she was journeying to a new horizon for herself. She had to find purpose beyond what had always been comfortable for her at Dunvegan. Finding the treasure of *Uamh Oir* would provide her with a new life, the purpose she sought, and the freedom she'd always wanted. With no one else responsible for her or her choices, and self-imposed exile in her own cottage, it meant she would never be hurt by others leaving her again.

With a renewed sense of determination, Rowena scanned the ship below for Marcus, to no avail. Only a few sailors scurried across the deck, and one stood on the forecastle, manning the tiller. Rowena frowned. Was Marcus below deck?

She pulled her shawl tightly about herself to keep out the damp morning air and sea spray, and with her feet braced, she leaned against the railing, watching the activity below as more sailors reappeared topside, most likely relieving the night watch.

As the salty air rejuvenated her, Rowena relaxed into the moment. Before she knew it, the sun rose higher in the morning sky and the rough waters calmed, rocking the boat gently. Open water stretched in every direction she looked. Instead of the disquieting feeling she would have expected, the isolation brought her a sense of peace. Rowena closed her eyes and listened to the song of the wind stirring the sea.

Back at Dunvegan she'd always felt restless and without any particular direction. Her brothers loved her but failed to either understand her or guide her in any way. Most likely because they'd been absent during her formative years. Yet today, she felt herself changing, though she could not say precisely how except that she felt stronger, more in control of her life. Rowena opened her eyes and smiled. She was happier, too, happier than she had been for a very long time. Was it because for the first time in her life she felt she had a purpose?

Leaning her elbows upon the railing, she gazed at the green water. The voices of the crew working below blended together into a low and steady hum. Rowena blocked out the noise, concentrating on the water, allowing her mind to be at peace.

A sharp noise from above crashed through her thoughts. Rowena straightened, looking for the source of the noise. From out of nowhere a huge black form swung from the sky, aimed straight for her head. Before she could react, she felt a strong pair of hands about her waist. She fell backwards, hitting the wooden deck with a thump. A suffocating weight enveloped her. She could not move, could not breathe.

Desperately, she clawed at the cold, wet canvas that pinned her to the deck. An ominous tearing sound rent the air and the cloth surrounding her went slack. She hauled in a breath of the salty air, grateful to once again be staring at the morning sky.

"Rowena?" Marcus pushed the heavy canvas aside, then stood. "Are you unharmed?" he asked as he sheathed his *sgian-dubh*.

"I—I believe so." Rowena accepted Marcus's outstretched hand and he helped her to her feet. He pulled away, but a sudden trembling overcame her limbs, leaving her unable to stand on her own. He pulled her against him once more. "What happened?"

"The mainsail broke free. It must have been damaged in the early morning storm." He studied her, deep concern drawing his brows together. "Are you certain you are well?"

She nodded. "Where did you come from? I came up here to search for you and could find you nowhere on deck."

"It was the changing of the watch. I only came above deck a few moments ago. When I saw you standing at the rail, I was on my way to you just as the sail collapsed. I'm grateful I came topside when I did." His voice sounded strained.

"So am I," she said as her trembling eased. Rowena took a step back, out of his arms, and gazed at the man who had saved her. His dark eyes held concern, but also kindness and understanding, reflecting what she had always known. This was a man she could trust. From the day they had met, she had always known there was goodness in Marcus's heart despite the fact he was a MacDonald.

She managed a smile. "Thank you, for today, and for all the other times you were always there when I needed you."

"I blame myself for your misfortune." He clenched his jaw. "I should have been with you."

"You had no idea I had left our quarters. Besides, you cannot be with me at all times on this voyage. You are the captain. Your duty is to the ship, not me."

"As far as others are concerned, you are my wife. I would be a poor husband if the first day of this voyage ended your life or tossed you over that rail."

Over the rail. Rowena tensed and her trembling ceased. "Where is Bryce?"

They were interrupted when several crewmen scrambled onto the deck, enquiring about her condition.

"We tried tae warn ye, milady, when the mainsail sagged, but ye must nae have heard our calls," a tall, lanky young man explained, his eyes wide in his youthful face. He couldn't be more than ten and seven years of age.

Rowena looked at the four crewmen who had gathered upon the quarterdeck. They were all young. The eldest couldn't have been more than a score and two. None of them could have been experienced sailors, except for the man Marcus had called Eck, who joined the group gathered about the sail. Even then, Eck was no more than a score and ten. No wonder Marcus felt such a compelling need to make settlements on his men's families. They would have been in the prime of their lives, and their families had lost a source of income for years to come.

"Thank you for trying to warn me," Rowena replied with a penitent smile. "I was caught up in my own thoughts. I will pay more attention when I am on deck in the future."

The young men nodded. They set about gathering the sail in order to repair the damage to the canvas.

Eck remained a few moments more, whispering something to Marcus before he also departed. "I am pleased to see you unharmed, Mrs MacDonald."

Rowena startled at the use of her married name. It was the first time she'd heard those words in connection with herself. She must not get used to them, for they would not be hers for long.

Marcus turned swiftly back to Rowena. "Why did you ask about Bryce?"

"He mentioned last night that I should take care so that I did not fall overboard."

Marcus's face hardened. "Eck reports that Bryce was unwillingly swabbing the forecastle for the past hour, under Thomas's supervision."

Rowena's jaw sagged. "You had him swabbing a deck in the middle of a storm?"

Marcus's features softened and the hint of a smile pulled up the corner of his mouth. "What better way to break him, than to give him an impossible task? Bryce has a few lessons to learn before he will be a functioning member of this crew."

Rowena held back a smile. Marcus would not humiliate his cousin, but he would teach him the value of hard work as a part of his crew. "I'm ready to get started on my own contributions. Would you show me to the treasure?"

"You should first break your fast." His smile vanished. "The food aboard is nothing like Mrs Honey's, I'm afraid."

"I didn't expect it to be. Whatever is good enough for the rest of you is good enough for me."

A glint of admiration brightened his eyes. "Come with

me. The galley and the treasure are below deck."

Rowena resettled her shawl about her shoulders and followed Marcus. Her new life was about to start. The thought filled her with a deep sense of satisfaction that she could do something to help her husband, and perhaps relieve him of some of the burden he had chosen to carry.

<hr />

MARCUS CLUTCHED A cabin lantern in his hand as he led Rowena down the fore hatch and to the port side. The galley was empty except for Bennett the cook who offered Rowena a slice of ham placed between two halves of a biscuit, and a small portion of ale. Food aboard the ship tended to be simple and salty, but she did not object. When she was through, they proceeded down to the ship's hold. The air below deck was stale and unmoving, yet any foul odour was offset by the scents of pitch, oakum, and wood. As his eyes adjusted to the semi-darkness, his gaze moved to Rowena.

Excitement lit her features and brought a sparkle to her eyes that rivalled any of the gems she would soon hold in her hands. The light from the lantern penetrated the gloom, bathing the hold in muted hues of yellow and gold. Revealed were cannon balls, the powder locker, casks of drinking water and ale, provision barrels containing beef on the port side, pork on the starboard side, and flour, potatoes, rice, and the like in the wings.

"This way," Marcus said as they walked past the brig and fore mast towards the bow of the ship. The berth deck was above them, next to the galley, but since the men were either asleep or above deck, the only noise around them was the lapping of water against the hull. At the door, he paused to open the iron padlock, then handed the skeleton key to Rowena. "You'll need this so that you may come to the treasury room whenever you like."

She accepted the iron key. "I am honoured."

"I trust you," he said with a smile.

Rowena frowned. "Why bring the treasure with you? Why not leave it at Dunvegan or somewhere safe on land?"

"We had no time to offload the treasure due to our hasty departure." Marcus opened the door and held back to allow Rowena to enter first.

She stepped inside and stopped, gazing spellbound, scarcely breathing.

"What do you think?" He set the lantern on a hook that hung from a beam overhead.

"I'm overwhelmed," she whispered, her voice filled with awe. "The treasure is so much larger than I had imagined."

Chests and barrels of jewels, silver, and gold filled the chamber. He lifted a large emerald from atop a chest near his feet. "With one of these stones you could buy a castle somewhere in the Highlands."

"There is so much here." She shook her head dazedly as her gaze wandered over piles of silver and gold bullion, barrels of gold coins, silver plates and vases studded with jewels, lustrous black pearls, diamonds, emerald, rubies, and sapphires. "You are going to give all this away to the families of the crewmen you lost?"

"Most of it. Close your eyes." He stepped farther into the chamber and retrieved a necklace that from the moment he'd seen it had reminded him of Rowena. He slipped the cold metal around her neck and fastened the lock, then arranged it to settle between the rise of her breasts. "You can open your eyes now."

Rowena did as requested, glanced down at her chest, and gasped. "Marcus. It's the most exquisite necklace I've ever seen." Her fingers came up to caress the largest square-cut emerald at the centre. It was surrounded by diamonds and had a large round diamond between each of the twenty other similarly designed square-cut emeralds of graduating size as they wrapped about her neck. Facets of the diamonds caught the lantern light and turned it into a dazzling array of brilliant hues that cascaded across the chamber.

"It matches your wedding ring," he said with a hint of pride.

A smile touched Rowena's lips. "It must be worth a fortune."

"It is worthy of a queen."

"I am no queen." Her smile faltered. The brilliance vanished from her eyes. "My future will never afford me the means to wear this." She reached up to remove it, but he stalled her, forcing her hands away and instead of pulling back, he ran his fingers through her hair. He brought the length forward to settle on either side of the necklace.

His fingers tingled as if they had been frozen and were now being painfully brought back to life. The thick, silky strands flowed through his fingers like warm honey. He wondered how the silkiness would feel against his naked chest.

He drew a slow deep breath, which did nothing to clear his thoughts. Instead, the tingling spread from his fingers to his wrists and arms. His loins ached; the muscles of his belly knotted. He shouldn't have touched her. The thought that he should pull back flashed through his mind. But instead of shifting away, he leaned down and his lips covered hers.

To his surprise, she did not struggle, but opened her lips, inviting him beyond, to taste, to sample, to plunder to his heart's content. His hands framed her face as he stepped closer, pressing his hardness against her melting softness.

Their lips melded, their tongues twined, sliding sensuously together as they once had. The kiss was as heady as any they'd ever shared. His compulsion to feed his hunger flared like a fever, growing more intense with every beat of his heart.

His fingers left her face to trail across her shoulders. One hand encircled her, pulling her more tightly against him, while the other traced the line of her hip. Rowena's hands in turn came up to his shoulders with one moving on to sink deep into the thickness of his hair.

Quivering excitement held him enthralled as every inch of his skin, every nerve thrummed with desire. Their kiss changed from hungry to ravenous. His senses leapt as he shifted his hand to her breast. Forcing the necklace aside, his fingers stroked, gently kneading. Beneath his touch, her breast swelled; her nipple tightened to a firm bud; and Rowena gasped and broke the kiss.

Through a haze of passion, Marcus stepped back. If he did not cease this madness right now, there would be no going back for him. He battled to block his desire even as need flared.

Rowena's breathing was as harsh as his own. Her eyes glazed with passion as he stared down at her rosy cheeks and swollen lips. A stubborn thought refused to abate: *She is my wife.* He should have the freedom to enjoy her at any opportunity that presented itself. He shot her a resigned glance. They both knew he could not. His future would take him in a direction that did not include her. "I did not mean to get so carried away," Marcus said, his voice deepened by desire and gravelly with frustration.

Drawing breath after breath until the rise and fall of her chest slowed to a normal rhythm, she met his gaze and held it. "I am as much at fault as you are. It will not happen again."

"I—"

"Captain, I am sorry to interrupt." A dark-haired crewman stepped through the open doorway of the treasury room.

"What do you need, Gordon?" Marcus asked, keeping his irritation in check. He hadn't said all he'd needed to say to Rowena.

Gordon shifted nervously on the balls of his feet. "Mr MacFarlane asked me to come get you. He said it is urgent."

Eck wouldn't have interrupted unless it truly was important. "Tell him I will be right there."

With a nod, Gordon left as silently as he had come. Marcus wondered for a moment how much of the exchange the young man had witnessed between himself and Rowena, even though it mattered little to the crew. As far as they knew, he was a newly married man who deserved a stolen moment here and there with his bride. "We will continue this conversation later," he said to Rowena, and with a frown, he headed towards a cabinet on the side of the chamber to unfold the hidden desktop. "You'll find paper, ink, and several quills in here. Help yourself to whatever you need."

He held her gaze for a moment more, until—jaw clenched—he turned and headed above deck, fighting the urge to go back and pull her into his arms once more.

CHAPTER ELEVEN

ARCUS EMERGED FROM below and headed towards the main deck. He was grateful for the whipping wind that soothed his overheated body and calmed his jumbled brain. The routine of life at sea had ever been a balm to his nerves, even during the hardships that had befallen the crew.

At his approach, Eck looked up from his inspection of the damaged sail. "I found something I wanted you to see before the men started their repairs." He pointed to a section of the rope at the bottom of the sail.

Marcus knelt on the deck of the ship and ran his hands over the sailcloth that had nearly knocked Rowena overboard. Something about the way it had pulled away from the rigging did not sit right with him. Though the storm they had just experienced this morning had been rough, he and Eck had known much worse. True, it wasn't unusual to lose a sail now and again, but he'd never seen the cording frayed quite like this.

Marcus looked across the canvas to his friend. A worried expression played across Eck's typically carefree countenance.

"What would sever a line this way?" Marcus asked, holding up the cord Eck had pointed out.

"The cut is too clean for a stress tear." Eck rolled the cable between his fingers. "I'd have to say a sharp blade." He tossed the rope onto the deck. "The idea of having a saboteur aboard this ship does not rest easy with me."

"That makes two of us." Marcus lifted his gaze from the cording. "You are certain Bryce was busy at the time of this accident?"

"I was personally watching him swab the deck. He could not have done this."

Marcus frowned. That meant someone else, one of his own men or one of the nine he'd taken on from the Mac-Leods, was responsible. He could still recall the whole scene. He had just returned to the deck when the sail had let loose. If he had not witnessed it, and run faster than he ever had before in order to knock Rowena to the ground . . .

"I know that look." Eck's voice broke into Marcus's thoughts. "You are not responsible for Rowena's accident."

"Aye, I am. I should have been with her."

Eck lifted a brow. "As captain of this ship it is impossible to be with her day and night. Besides, from what I've seen of your bride, she seems more resilient than most women."

"As her husband it is my duty to protect her."

"Duty or desire? Three days ago you did not want a wife. Now you have one." Eck's gaze ran over him in cool appraisal. "I've never known you to be indecisive about anything.

The crew and I need you to be fully committed to our current voyage. The dangers are great and the crew is on edge from our previous misfortune. It would be best if you focused your attention on them until we successfully retrieve the treasure with no casualties. Then, once that is through, all your thoughts can turn to desire and that lovely bride of yours."

"You are right." Marcus looked beyond where they stood, watching the forenoon watch change places with the morning watch. "The crew needs more observation than Rowena does. Gold obviously did not buy loyalty from some of them. One of them severed that rope. I need to find out if that action was directed at Rowena, or if someone wants to disrupt our attempt to retrieve the secrets deep within the Cave of Gold."

"We should reach our destination by this evening."

"Any chance we could slow our journey down and give me a chance to figure out who amongst us might be the saboteur?"

"Our journey is already slowed without our mainsail." Eck shrugged. "I could tell the men to repair this sail instead of raising a spare."

Marcus nodded. "That would be best. It gives us both time to observe the goings-on of this crew."

"Aye, aye, Captain." Eck smiled and saluted his friend. "I'll find us the longest route possible to our destination."

"I will start by casually interviewing the men and seeing

if any of them hold a grudge against me or, as you said, the misfortune that has befallen us lately." Picking up the gauntlet of his new challenge, Marcus turned and strode towards the men gathered about the mainmast, discussing the damaged and missing sail. He'd start his interviews with them and do everything possible to keep his mind from drifting back to the woman in the treasure room two decks below.

BRYCE LEANED BACK against the railing of the main deck, released a deep, gratified sigh, and looked at the deck he'd finished swabbing for the second time. Now that the storm had eased, he'd made real progress. The wood was not only clean, it shone from his efforts. He'd had no idea that swabbing the deck with saltwater kept the wood watertight and the mould and fungus away until that bossy first mate had told him.

He hadn't expected to have to work on the ship while they sailed to retrieve his treasure. At first, he'd been furious to have to stoop to the level of every other man on this ship and he'd let everyone around him know that fact. But while he'd been swabbing, his anger had faded and a sense of accomplishment had filled him. Bryce would never tell his cousin he had liked the hard, physical work.

In the fold of his own clan, he'd never felt like that. He

was always too clumsy, too slow, too timid. Today when he'd worked amongst the others, he'd felt a part of something bigger. The other men had laughed, making him the brunt of many jokes while he'd been swabbing away the swells that had come over the railing, but none of the jokes had been personal, only about the futility of the task. After the seas had settled, they'd complimented him on his perseverance.

No one had ever acknowledged him in such a manner before. In turn, he had worked harder, until he'd finished the entire upper deck of the ship from bow to stern. Bryce's gaze shifted to the men overhead on the riggings and to those on the forecastle with the maps and charts and sextant. They knew how to man this ship, and suddenly Bryce wanted that more than even the treasure they would soon retrieve. He'd never been that good with a sword, but perhaps he could learn how to work aboard a ship. He frowned. Would his cousin allow such a thing? Bryce hadn't exactly endeared himself to the man with his prior actions.

Perhaps if he swabbed the deck again, Marcus would see he was willing to do menial tasks with pride, so that perhaps he could move on to others with more responsibility. Gathering his pail of saltwater, he started swabbing one more time.

IT HAD HAPPENED again. Rowena watched Marcus leave the hold and disappear into the darkness beyond. How could she have let Marcus kiss her again?

She smothered a groan. What was she going to do? There had always been an overbright attraction between them. Denying that it existed was getting both of them nowhere. For their current arrangement to be successful, they had to keep each other at arm's length and Marcus had to stop giving her gifts worthy of a queen.

Or, another voice inside her countered, *give in to the temptation.* She paused. Once tasted, would the desire between them burn out as quickly as it always came over them? She had her doubts, but it was something that deserved consideration.

More confused about Marcus than ever, Rowena reached up and unfastened the heavy necklace, fingering once more the emeralds that were bigger than any she'd ever seen before. He'd wanted her to keep this one treasure for herself, but how could she when every time she looked upon the priceless gems she would think of Marcus and remember their breath-stealing kisses?

How could she not, when its value could pay for an entire new life, a whole new freedom?

She would have no need of something so refined in her new life after this voyage had ended. It would make far more sense for her to sell off the emeralds one at a time as a means of income over the coming years, yet she doubted she could do that either. Marcus meant too much to her to destroy the only thing he had ever given her that had been his own. Her gaze dropped to her wedding ring and the winking emerald there. He'd given her a symbol of his love and affection that wasn't true. When their marriage was annulled, her mother's ring would be returned to Alastair and at least that wrong would be righted.

With a sigh, Rowena placed the necklace amongst the treasure once more. Perhaps while she was counting gold coins she would think of a solution to keep herself from reacting every time Marcus drew near.

At the desk, she withdrew a sheet of parchment and placed it on the flat surface of the desk, dipped a quill in ink and wrote in script *An Inventory of the Treasure of Marcus MacDonald*. She tipped over one of the barrels of coins and watched as the gold pieces jostled across each other to settle at her feet. Then, using the barrel as a seat, she started counting.

Hours later she was so engrossed in her calculations that she startled when the lantern extinguished and the door of the treasury snapped closed, pitching the chamber into total darkness. "Nay," she cried first with shock, then with a flash of agitation as uncounted coins slipped from her fingers. She'd have to recount her most recent barrel all over again.

With an effort not to trip over the haphazardly stored loot, she made her way to the door and gave a tug on the handle, only to find it had been locked from the outside and she had the only key inside the chamber. It might take hours before Marcus took notice of her absence.

A shiver of fear raced down her spine. This was the second time something strange had happened to her on this ship since they'd set sail. Someone or something did not want her on this vessel.

Her grip tightened on the handle, and she gave it a hard shake. "Is anyone out there? Can you hear me?" Her stomach clenched. The treasury was far back in the bow of the ship— too far away from the main areas of the vessel for anyone to hear her. With shaking fingers, she shook the door handle again. She knew her efforts were futile but rattling the door helped keep her mind off her fear. She'd seen the lock from the outside. It was stout and no matter how ruthlessly she rattled the door, the lock would hold.

With a sigh of frustration, she released the door handle as despondency set in, weakening her limbs, and forcing her to find her way back to the tipped barrel. She would have to wait for either the person who locked her in to come back and finish her off, or for someone to free her. Her eyes had adjusted to the darkness enough for her to make out dark shapes but no detail. But just to be prepared, she rummaged for a pile of gold and silver bullion she'd seen earlier. When her fingers closed around something heavy and hard, she lifted it, then placed it in her lap. Better to be prepared in case . . .

When a soft clink of coins sounded behind her, Rowena

stiffened. Could someone or something still be in there with her? Rowena's heart raced at the thought, as she held her breath listening for any sound other than the waves lapping against the hull. She heard nothing, and she settled in to wait. She'd already ruled out anything supernatural extinguishing the lantern's flame. Her experience with her mother had taught her there were telltale signs when a spirit was near. She'd felt no chill, seen no mist, felt no otherworldly presence.

A real person had done this. Someone who was light of foot and quick of hand. She thought back to when she'd first boarded the ship and had seen four men high above on the footropes as they prepared to lower the sail. They had to be not only strong, but also light-footed. Perhaps one of them did not want their current voyage to succeed or were adamantly opposed to a female aboard their ship.

A sudden flush of heat came to her cheeks as anger knotted her stomach. She had as much right to be on this ship as any of the men aboard. Rowena reached down and picked up a handful of coins. She flung one at the pile, hearing it bounce off the other coins, and then flung a second and a third.

After she'd lost count of the number of coins she'd thrown back into the pile, she instead reached down and let them trickle through her fingers until it was silent in the chamber once more. As proven by the vastness of the treasure these men had already recovered, they were earning more as treasure seekers than they would ever earn in a lifetime on land. Why would they want to cease their plundering when a guaranteed treasure waited for them at their next destination?

The only logical answer was that someone objected to her presence on *The Cliodna*. The fear that resided in Rowena's chest shifted to a slow-burning anger. Was it Bryce who didn't want to share any of his ill-gotten gains? Or one of the crew? It didn't matter because as soon as she was released from this gaol, she would take it upon herself to find out who wanted her out of the way. She might be female, but she was not powerless.

If someone wanted her dead, perhaps it was time to stop resisting the attraction between herself and her husband. She could go to her grave having tasted what else lay behind his passionate kisses. If she lived, then she could still petition for an annulment from someone who would not require a physical examination as part of those proceedings. Or, they could remain married, and live their lives separated by two distinct goals and dreams.

She sighed into the emptiness of the chamber and clutched the heavy bullion in her hands. It appeared she would have plenty of time to consider her options while she waited for whatever happened next.

CHAPTER TWELVE

MARCUS OPENED HIS cabin door and looked inside the chamber, expecting to see Rowena sitting at the table or on the bed. She wasn't there. With a frown he grabbed a brace of candles from the table and raced from the room. When she'd missed the midday meal, he had figured she was simply too engrossed in her work to realise the passage of time, or that she had been avoiding him after he'd stolen yet another kiss. Then she'd missed supper. Now the sun was starting to set, and he couldn't shake the feeling that something else had happened. He'd check the hold first before he raised an alarm, and if she wasn't there, he'd make every crewman on this ship search every corner of the vessel until she was found.

Darkness blanketed everything inside the bowels of the ship, but he knew this place like the back of his hand. Once he passed the powder locker, he lit the candles with flint and steel and scanned the hold and, seeing nothing, he hurried to the treasury. The door was locked and no light emanated from inside the chamber. He was about to turn away when he heard the shifting of coins. "Rowena?"

"Marcus, I'm in here." Footstep shuffled towards the door. "Help me get out of here."

"What happened here?" He rattled the lock.

He heard a relieved rush of breath on the opposite side of the door. "Someone locked me inside after extinguishing the lantern." Her voice held anger but a hint of desperation.

"You've been in the dark this whole time?" His throat went dry as he rattled the lock again. He had to find a way inside.

"Do you have another key?" she asked in a hopeful voice softened by the thickness of the door between them.

"I gave you the only one." He set the candelabra down, crouching to feel along the bottom of the door where it met the floor. There wasn't enough space for her to slip the key underneath to him. He sat back on his heels. "I have an idea. Move away from the door."

When Marcus heard her shuffle away, he stood and drew his sword. He might not be able to cut through the metal lock, but he could cleave through the door. Lifting his sword high, he brought the weapon down at an angle once, twice, three times before the wood splintered and the padlock and a chunk of the door fell to the floor.

He sheathed his sword and opened the door. The dim candlelight cast a surreal cloak of grey across the treasury. Rowena stepped from the shadows. "Thank you for coming for me," she said, her face pale and grim in the mellow light. "I believe someone doesn't want me aboard this ship."

"Tell me what happened." He moved towards her, his gait measured and steady. He wanted more than anything to pull her against his chest, to comfort her. However, the next time they touched, he wanted her to be the one to initiate it.

"I was taking inventory and must have been thoroughly engrossed in my counting because I heard not a sound when suddenly the light extinguished and the door closed."

"I've been interviewing the men all morning and afternoon, trying to discern who amongst us might have tampered with the sail. And now this."

A slight widening of her eyes suggested she suspected foul play might have been involved in both incidents as well. "Did you come to any conclusions?"

A long pause settled between them until only the sound of the waves against the hull echoed around them. The steady rhythm had most likely helped to keep Rowena calm during her hours in the darkness. "I've narrowed the list to four people: Bryce, Rob Roy, Gordon, and Fergus."

She walked up before him, tipping her head back. "How will we determine who amongst the four is trying to kill me?"

"We?" His brows rose in challenge.

"Aye. We. I have a stake in the outcome, therefore I should be part of the investigation."

"Nay." He had no intention of letting her involve herself in anything that might cause her more difficulty. "It could be dangerous."

She raised a brow. "More dangerous than having a sail almost knock you overboard or being locked in a dark chamber for hours on end, waiting for your attacker to come back and finish his task?"

"The matter is being dealt with. Rest assured of that."

Her glare pierced him. "Has anyone ever told you that you are insufferable?"

"More than I'd like."

The comment robbed her of words long enough for him to study her more closely. She appeared unharmed from her time alone and her tongue was as sharp as it had ever been. Instead of smiling at the thought, his brows drew together when his gaze lowered to her bosom, rising and falling with the force of her indignation. "Where is the necklace I gave you?"

She pointed to a chest behind her. "I cannot keep it, so I returned it the chest over there."

"Over where?"

She turned to look at where she'd set the priceless jewellery. Her eyes went wide. "It's gone. Whoever was down here with me must have taken it with them after they extinguished the light."

"Then whoever has the necklace in his possession is the person we are looking for."

"We?" she asked, no doubt hoping he had changed his mind.

Marcus set his jaw. The woman before him was certainly

different than the one he'd left behind all those months ago. She had suffered four personal attacks in the past two days, and yet she seemed eager to continue placing herself in danger. "We, meaning my first mate and myself. Eck and I will conduct a search for the missing necklace. You will return to our cabin and stay put. Until we figure out who is trying to harm you, you'll remain where it is safe."

ROWENA FOLLOWED MARCUS back to their cabin even though she did not intend to stay there long. She'd been locked in a dark chamber all day. If he thought she would willingly submit to being locked up again, then he did not know her well at all.

Once Marcus left to attend to his duty as captain, Rowena opened her trunk and withdrew the leather tunic and trousers Fiona had given her. Rowena fingered the supple leather garments that had at one time belonged to her ancestor, Leona MacLeod, who had been gifted them by the fairies. Only someone who had a special relationship with the fairies could wear the garments.

Rowena's hand stilled. She'd been raised on the same fairy stories as her brothers, and as a MacLeod it was difficult not to believe in the magic of the Fairy Flag. *Am Bratach Sith*, the priceless artifact, had been given to them by the fairies and could only be used to rescue the clan from defeat three times. However, the fairy garments were a gift given with no restricting limits because of their MacLeod ancestor's special relationship with the fairies. Only women who shared a similar bond as their ancestor could wear the tunic and trousers created with fairy magic.

The leather garments had protected Fiona during their recent battles with the MacDonalds and the English. Would the fairy-softened leather help Rowena? She stood and set the garments on the bed and started to undress. First she had to find out if the garments would accept her since she hadn't had time before they'd left Dunvegan. Fairy blood ran in her veins. Would that be enough for the fairies to approve of her wearing them? Rowena pressed her lips into a thin line. Only one way to find out.

Dressed only in her drawers and her stays, she slipped first one leg then the other into the trousers, pulled them up to her waist, and tied them closed. The leather moulded to her curves, cold at first, then warming to the temperature of her skin as she waited to see what might happen next. Fiona had said she would experience great pain if the fairies did not approve.

Rowena's breath stilled and every muscle tensed as a long moment passed, and then another. When nothing happened, she relaxed. It seemed fairy blood was enough to qualify her to wear the special garments. Quickly, she slipped into the tunic and lashed it closed.

For a moment she considered wearing her dress over the

leather garments but then dismissed the idea. If someone objected to her presence on this ship because she was female, then perhaps dressing like a man would help her blend in. With a nod of satisfaction, she returned to her trunk to retrieve the package Mrs Honey had sent with her. The cook at Dunvegan always said the way to a man's heart was through his stomach. Armed with the weapon of Mrs Honey's choosing, Rowena opened the cabin door and headed for the galley. It was time for her to put that old adage to the test with the other five-and-fifty men aboard this ship. And perhaps if one of them reacted oddly to her gift, she might know who had locked her in the treasury.

In the galley, the cook was more than happy to supply her with the ale she requested when she offered him a piece of shortbread with candied citrus mixed in. The sweet treat was one of Mrs Honey's specialties and Rowena had loved the buttery Scottish delicacy since she was a child. The cook accompanied her above deck, carrying a casket of ale.

At the sight of the ale, the men above deck turned towards the two of them. The second dogwatch had ended, and the night watch began at eight in the evening, meaning many of the men were already above deck. The crew were usually only allotted a portion of ale before noon and another at the end of their working day, though they usually took their ale below deck in the galley with a piece of salted fish and hard tack. Tonight Rowena had something else planned for them.

When the shock of her presence subsided, the deck was silent except for the gusting of the wind and the motion of the waves. The gazes slid along her form. Rowena lifted her chin and straightened, warding off the feeling that they were judging her. "I brought sweets from home for you all. Come, there is enough for two shortbreads apiece. And the cook has agreed to double your portion of ale for tonight."

Cheers arose as the men came forward to collect their refreshments. They lined up and accepted shortbread and ale. Many graced her with smiles and thanks. All except the man the cook identified as Gordon. He approached her with a scowl. Then after accepting his portion with a grumbled "thanks," he stepped back to the railing, piercing her with his angry gaze.

Rowena swallowed against a sudden tightness in her throat. Gordon had come below to tell Marcus he was needed on deck. He knew she had been in the treasury. It seemed likely he was also the one who had locked her in that chamber. Gordon's eyes narrowed, the hate in them as sharp as a newly honed blade.

She forced herself to breathe and look away, wishing she hadn't when she saw Marcus striding towards her from the quarterdeck, his green eyes blazing every bit as much as Gordon's.

He moved to the front of the line, forcing Bryce who was next up aside. "What are you doing out of our cabin?" His gaze dropped to her chest, moving down to her waist and hips before returning to her face. "What are you wearing?"

She avoided the second question. "I am sharing a delight Mrs Honey prepared for your crewmen." Rowena offered Marcus two shortbread. "Try them. They are quite delicious."

He ignored the proffered treat. "You belong where it is safe," he said in a lowered tone.

"Is anywhere truly safe on this ship?" she asked with an arched brow. "That is why I changed into these leather garments. They will protect me in ways you cannot."

He scowled. "That garment reveals your every curve. How am I to protect you when you wear such a tantalising thing?"

Warmth coiled in her stomach. He thought her tantalising? She set the shortbread aside then tipped her face up to his, noting the strong lines of his jaw and the strength of his neck and shoulders. "It is protective armour." She spread her arms, as though offering her armoured chest for review. "Strike me with your blade and you will see of what I speak." The armour had protected Fiona. She hoped it would do the same for her.

"I will do no such thing."

From behind him, Bryce stepped out and lunged forward, dagger in hand. He struck directly above her heart.

Rowena gasped at the surprise attack, releasing her breath a heartbeat later when the tip of his blade did not penetrate the supple leather.

The crew gasped.

In that same moment, Marcus yanked Bryce from her, sending him to the wooden deck in a massive display of strength. "How dare you strike my wife," Marcus growled as he left Bryce on the deck and returned to her side, catching her to him with an arm under her breast. "She is mine. No one shall touch Rowena other than me. Do you all understand?"

The crewmen nodded, even Gordon. Rowena forced herself to breathe as the feel of Marcus's grip against her ribs limited the expansion of her lungs.

"I was not attacking her to be malicious," Bryce said, standing once more. "I trusted that she was serious about the armour protecting her and that she would come to no harm." He looked about at the others gathered. "We all wanted to know if the armour worked."

Marcus's eyes blazed. "And what if Rowena's claim had been wrong and your blade pierced her chest? What then?"

"I did not think beyond the strike." Bryce's shoulders slumped as he turned his gaze to Rowena. "I'm sorry."

The fight seemed to leave Marcus at the apology as his hold on her relaxed. "That was a dangerous thing to do, Rowena."

"It proved my point. This armour is infused with fairy magic. Wearing it will protect me from physical harm."

His scowl deepened. "From a blade perhaps, but I doubt it will keep you from drowning if someone knocks you overboard."

She hadn't considered that, though she wasn't ready to go back to the cabin without finishing what she had started. "Help me pass out the remainder of the shortbread and ale then I will go back."

She could see he wanted to refuse yet knew he could not. Instead, he grabbed the shortbread and handed them back to her. "Continue. I'll remain by your side until you are done here."

She nodded and returned to handing out the shortbread. By now, word had spread to those men below deck that something unusual was happening above, and even those who had been sleeping came to gather their refreshments.

The last person to gather their evening treat was the man Marcus called Eck. He hesitated taking the shortbread when his gaze lit upon her momentarily before covering his response with a brilliant smile. While she helped the cook clean up, she stepped away from Marcus and Eck, but was close enough to hear the two men talking.

"What a lovely sight to behold, especially her arse. From now on I think lasses should wear trousers," Eck murmured, ceasing his observation at Marcus's harsh glare.

"That's my wife you are ogling."

"Then I suggest you take her back to your quarters and stake your claim."

"It's not that easy, you fool," Marcus ground out.

Eck shrugged. "All of your professions of duty and penance might have held up before you married the girl. But I can see since you returned from Dunvegan with your bride in tow that you are a changed man."

Marcus opened his mouth to reply but Eck continued. "Deny it all you want, my friend. You are a changed man since Rowena has come into your presence again. So I say either stop the charade and bed her or let some other man have her. That doesn't seem like a tough choice to me."

Marcus turned to stare at her for a moment, his gaze moving over her like a lover's soft caress. As he strode to her, her breath caught and heat warmed her blood. "What was it you hoped to accomplish by plying the men with ale and sweet treats?"

He looped his arm through hers and turned her towards the captain's quarters. "I thought it was the best way to see if any of the men reacted negatively to me."

She heard him grunt. "Other than Bryce, did any of them?"

"I doubt Bryce would have stabbed me, especially in front of the others if I had not encouraged it. He had plenty of opportunity to do me in before we set foot on this ship."

Marcus grunted again. "You're probably right about that."

"One man did have an interesting response."

At the cabin door, Marcus stopped to open it, allowing her to move past him. "Who?"

"Your cook identified him as Gordon."

Marcus nodded. He turned back towards the door. "Eck and I will take care of this. I'll sleep better tonight knowing he is in the brig."

With a hand on his arm, Rowena stopped Marcus from leaving. "I am safe enough tonight in your company. Let him believe he has succeeded in sending me into banishment in your chamber."

"Our chamber." He left the door and turned back to her until there was only a small gap between their bodies. He inhaled, his nostrils flaring as he slid his hands down her back, across the supple leather, until he reached the curve of her hips. He lifted her slightly. The impact of his hardness impressed on her body and her mind, sending a jolt of desire to her very core.

Rowena held back a groan, wondering why they were fighting what had always been so natural between them. On the ship and in such close quarters, avoiding each other was near to impossible. There was no middle ground for them any longer.

She had to decide.

CHAPTER THIRTEEN

ROWENA LOOKED UP into Marcus's beautiful green eyes then pressed up on her toes. She held her breath as he bent his head to hers. Instead of kissing her, he pressed his forehead against her own, their lips so close and yet still not touching. His breath whispered against her lips, causing her heart to pound all the harder as the treasure they both wanted hung there between them. He was waiting for her, she suddenly realised. He would hold himself in this breathless torment until she initiated the kiss.

His fingers slipped around her neck, caressing her spine. "Rowena—" Her name spilled from his lips like the sound of a breeze across the deck of the ship, sending a stab of yearning to the core of her being. It was too late to pull back. Too late to stop whatever came next. She closed her eyes and leaned into him, slanting her face until her lips touched his as naturally as if they'd kissed each other a thousand times.

His lips were warm and firm and fit beautifully against her own. As he slid his lips against hers, reason washed away in a heated tide. Everything that divided them—their clans, their goals—seemed inconsequential as he deepened the kiss.

Each thrust of his tongue evoked stunningly sharp reverberations deep in her womb. The kiss became the centre of her consciousness, all she knew or felt, even as she cursed it and craved it with equal measure.

Releasing a shuddering breath, Rowena surrendered. The protective walls she had built around her heart had been slashed open and could never be sealed again.

His lips left her mouth to brush across her throat. She arched her neck, giving him full access to her sensitive flesh. Marcus's hand rode the curve of her ribcage until his fingers came around to cup her breast. His thumb circled, caressing the ripening peak beneath her leather tunic. Rowena gasped as heat spread from his fingertips across her covered skin. And suddenly the leather armour that kept his touch from her flesh seemed too oppressive. She pulled back and reached for the lacing.

"Allow me." His voice was low and gravelly, already choked with desire. His fingers brushed hers away and he began to pull the laces. He peeled the leather from her then made short work of the stays beneath, tossing the cambric garment to the floor before reaching for the ties on her leather trousers and drawers. She'd never had anyone undress her before—not even a maid—as she'd always cared for herself. With Marcus standing so close, she could feel the heat of his skin and the growing bulge of his arousal against her naked flesh. She moved against him, blatantly inviting, her body demanding the intimate touch they longed to share.

He stared down at her, his green eyes dark with passion—passion she had ignited, passion that turned every muscle in his body to hard-edged steel. "No regrets?" he asked, his breathing unsteady.

"Not a one."

He released her and in the moonlight and shadows of the chamber removed his garments then captured her lips once more.

Need and desire infused her, and him, potent and real. She could feel it as his lips moved against hers, as he ran his hands down her back to cup her buttocks. As the blood in her veins turned to quicksilver, he broke the kiss and lowered his head, capturing first one peaked nipple in his mouth then the other. She raked her hands into his hair, pulling him even closer, reeling from the effects of this new intoxication. He'd asked about regrets; if she had any, it would be that they had waited so long to come together as one.

His fingers traced the line of her waist then feathered across her hips, his tongue following in the same molten path until he sank down on his knees before her. His hands on her thighs, his thumbs stroked the dark thatch of downy curls at her apex. He parted her and probed the tender flesh as his mouth pressed against her and his tongue delved inside with the same determined boldness he'd used to conquer her elsewhere.

Rowena stiffened at the intimate touch. She wanted to

pull away but then pressure gripped her and with a groan she surrendered to the need that flared deep inside. Caught in passion's grip, her knees grew weak. She slipped to the floor in front of Marcus, her mouth searching feverishly for his, her tongue greedy for the taste and feel of him.

He let her explore every hardened plane of his body before he drew her to her feet, then lifted her in his arms, carrying her to the bed. He placed her in the centre then settled beside her. Their bodies came together again. Rowena revelled in the sinewy strength of his muscles and the devouring strength of his lips as they roved everywhere, explored every hollow and curve.

She savoured the silken skin beneath her palms as she found the hardness that pressed against her and greedily stroked, branding him as hers. Her bold strokes wrenched a groan of pure ecstasy from him. A heartbeat later, he moved over her, spreading her thighs and settling between them. With gentleness he entered her, tearing away the last fragile protest of her body until her warmth clutched his.

A groan escaped her as she surrounded him fully, deep within. Nothing had ever felt so right, so natural. She stared up into his eyes, into the unwavering, unshakable green, and felt herself reeling as he moved in and out of her in a rhythm that was slow at first then built to a more frenetic pace, just like the rest of their lovemaking. They had been denied this intimacy so long that neither of them were in control of themselves or their responses.

Opening herself as she never had before, Rowena gloried in the pleasurable feel of his muscular body pressing her back against the mattress, his hips pinning her as he drove deep within her over and over again. She thrashed her head from side to side as she began to quake with mindless urgency born of fire and flame. An all-consuming sensation filled her as she neared the edge of a precipice. She twined her legs around Marcus's hips, fusing their bodies together as they rushed headlong over the brink of erupting glory.

Spent, he slumped upon her. A quiet, tender moment ticked past. She could feel his heart racing, felt the same tempo in her own chest as their heartbeats gradually slowed and their breathing steadied.

Finally, with a heaved breath, he withdrew and moved to settle at her side, pulling her against him as if he wasn't yet ready to release her fully. They lay there, staring up at the carved canopy. As silence enveloped them a surge of emotion swelled inside Rowena. She nestled her cheek against Marcus's, her hand drifting over the solid wall of his chest in a slow, sleepy caress until she closed her hand around his. "That wasn't supposed to happen. Though I'm glad it did."

Marcus remained silent for a long while. Rowena was half-certain he had fallen asleep when he finally kissed the top of her head and said, "I did not mean to lose control like I did. I apologise. The next time we will take our time."

Heat infused her cheeks at the possibility of a next time. "Now we at least have this to share for as long as this adventure continues."

"You know this means there is no going back for us. We are now married in every sense of the word."

She shook her head. "I can still petition for an annulment. I will simply find a way to do so without a physical examination."

He sat up and looked down at her. "There is more to consider than ourselves."

She frowned. "What do you mean?"

"What if we created a bairn?"

Her tongue moistened suddenly dry lips. "We cannot have a babe together. I would never do such a thing—to bring a child into this world when both parents are not involved in his rearing." She sat up and crossed her arms about her waist as fear chased the last remnants of pleasure from her body. "My father did that to Callum, Keiran, and me. With our mother's death we were alone. Keiran paid the ultimate price, being taken by the fairies. But Callum and I were abandoned, with only each other to help us move from one day to the next."

Marcus's finger moved to her lips. "Fear not." A smile so beautiful it took her breath away lit his dark face. "I will always care for what is mine."

Rowena swallowed roughly. She knew Marcus would love and care for any child of his as he did the fallen crewmen from his ship. He would not let a babe suffer in any monetary way. But what about the more intimate things a child needed? A father to teach him about right and wrong, how to be brave and compassionate? How to know when to fight a battle or how to negotiate peace? To offer protection, devotion, stability?

She could teach a babe much, but some things were better coming from a father. Bryce was proof of that. Marcus and Bryce were from the same clan, had similar opportunities, yet Marcus had had his father's attention while Bryce had not.

"You have my promise that I will take care of you and our child, Rowena." He kissed her lips with a sweetness that rocked her to her core. He drew her into his arms and settled back upon the bed, nestling her close.

"Then if I am with child you would stay with me?"

His gaze when he looked down at her was grave. "I must honour my men above all else."

She threw off his hands and moved to the far side of the bed. "You will abandon us then." A bolt of panic zagged through her.

There was a flicker of anger in his green eyes. "Only temporarily. Until my task is complete. The consummation of our marriage has changed nothing in that respect."

She looked at him indignantly. "It has changed everything for me." Rowena scrambled off the bed, snatching the corner of the burgundy coverlet, holding it before her to hide her nakedness as she looked about for her clothing. She finally located a pile of her things near the door. Dropping the coverlet, she reached for her stays and drawers.

"Where are you going?" His voice lowered to a menacing softness.

"Anywhere but here."

His lips thinned. "Have you forgotten we are on a ship—a ship full of men who have considered ravishing you from the moment you set foot aboard?" He pulled the coverlet back and patted the space beside him. "Come back to bed. There is nowhere else for you to go."

She ran trembling fingers through her hair. He was right, of course, but she refused to let him know it as she continued to dress. Only when she was fully encased in her fairy armour did she make her way back to the bed. "Because, as you said, there is no other option. I will sleep here." She reached for the pillow he'd left on the table earlier that morning and placed it at the foot of the bed.

"You have every right to be angry with me, but I cannot abandon the families of the men I lost, just as I could never abandon a child we brought into this world. You have to understand that." His expression held uncertainty and vulnerability, two things he had never shown her before.

A sudden wave of tenderness lessened the frustration and disappointment inside her. "I might not like it, but I do understand," she said as she settled on the bed near his feet. "So where does that leave us?"

"It leaves us exactly where we are—on our way to find a treasure."

She sat up, facing him. She needed a portion of that treasure to fund her future life . . . and possibly the life of a future child. Tears stung her eyes. Why had she given in to temptation? Heat suffused her cheeks at the memory of their bodies joined, his face filled with desire as he moved within her. She cleared her throat to relieve it of tightness. He'd made his position perfectly clear. She had no choice but to be brave and struggle through her future alone. "You believe the treasure truly exists?" she asked softly.

"I do. The other treasures Jacob Thorne left us should be proof enough of that. But then again—" his expression became shuttered "—I can make no promises other than that I will not risk any life but my own to retrieve what might be hidden in the Cave of Gold."

Why did those words cause her such a wrenching pang? "I choose to believe the treasure is there and that it will come to us without any loss of life."

When he settled back against the bed, staring up at the carved canopy, she did the same. Moonlight bathed the chamber in silvery light.

"My only need for the treasure of *Uamh Oir* before tonight was to further fund the families of the men I lost and to keep Bryce from coming after the people I care about. Now I must believe in its existence for you and also any potential child."

A spasm of pain centred in her chest at his words. "I do not want you to feel obligated to me. This marriage was meant to be temporary. We both have dreams. Now mine might include caring for a child. Perhaps it's time to start remembering what those dreams are and working towards their fulfilment."

"I have no dreams, only commitments."

Rowena drew a sharp breath and continued her contemplation of the shadows above her head. Earlier this evening she might have considered Marcus had deeper feelings for her than he was ready to express. Not now. He saw her only as something to conquer and an obstacle that stood in his way.

A heaviness weighed her down. In the morning they would arrive at their destination. The sooner they found the treasure the better. Then both she and Marcus could move forward with their lives. As far as a child was concerned . . . God would not be so cruel, would he? A child would change everything for both of them. She wasn't about to give up on her own dreams just yet, not until she knew for certain if she was to bear a child or not. She would have her answer soon enough. All she had to do was be patient.

DURING THE NIGHT watch as the stars shone bright overhead, the other crewmen had finally allowed Bryce to do something other than swab the deck. Thomas had taken the new sailor under his wing and had showed him how to adjust the sails and rigging to accommodate a calmer wind, and had taught him how to safely scramble up the ratlines on the windward side.

At first, Bryce's chest had been filled with jealousy over the fact these men had been trained by others to perform their duty, most likely by his own cousin. But after countless attempts to gain a toehold on the footropes while the ship swayed, that jealousy had slid into determination. And, after several successful attempts to reach the crow's nest and the yard where the solid wood post met the main mast, he released a cry of triumph into the darkness of night.

For the first time in his life, he had not proven bad at something. In fact, Thomas had said Bryce possessed a talent that only needed refining.

A talent. Never had Bryce heard those words associated with himself before.

For the remainder of his shift, Bryce worked harder than he'd ever worked in his life, feeling a deep sense of not only accomplishment, but also belonging. Such a feeling was new to him, but he intended to hold on to it for as long as he possibly could.

CHAPTER FOURTEEN

MARCUS WOKE IN the early morning light to the sound of a contented sigh. He sat up. Rowena lay in her fairy armour on top of the coverlet, her hair an unbound glory of lustrous dark brown shot with gold. Her eyes were closed, her lashes arcing on to the softness of her cheeks. Her pink lips were slightly parted. As he looked at her, the muscles of his belly knotted and his manhood hardened. The scent of heather radiated from her pale skin, shining in the pinkish-yellow light as though it had been sculpted by a loving hand.

A pang of tenderness shot through him. She had initiated their lovemaking last night. He'd thought that finally satiating what he'd wanted and had denied himself for so long would ease his desire. The rigidness of his manhood told him otherwise. He wanted Rowena every bit as much in the light of day as he had last night.

Marcus wrinkled his brows. He'd always thought that if this moment would come, he'd be able to take his pleasure and walk away. Yet he'd been the one to raise the subject of a possible pregnancy last night. A bairn would bind them together for a lifetime. Is that what he wanted? He had a duty to his men that he would move heaven and earth to fulfil, but what came after that?

The task might take months, years even. He'd claimed that he didn't want to tie Rowena to him when his future was still so uncertain. And still he had not only wedded her, he'd bedded her, tying her to him in ways that would be difficult to unravel. Even so, when he'd mentioned a child, after the shock had worn off, she had started planning how she could live a life with her child. A life that did not include him.

All her life Rowena had been forced to trust only herself. She'd had no one else to rely on. In some outlandish way he felt as though the bairn of which they spoke was already a reality and that she was stealing both it and herself from him. With a harsh groan, Marcus got out of bed.

God's blood! What did he want? To pay his debts? Learn to dream with Rowena? Bring a child into this world? He couldn't have all three. Somehow he had to find a solution. He slipped his arms into his shirt and his legs into his breeches. He would never find those answers here, staring down at the woman he wanted to pull into his arms more than he wanted to draw his next breath.

Marcus slid into his boots and opened the door of his chamber even as he tucked in his shirt. His expression tight and grim, he shut the door. He needed to find Gordon and discover why he'd threatened Rowena's life. Perhaps if

Marcus took out some of his frustration on the young lad, he might get the answers he needed more easily. He would never harm a member of his crew, but that didn't mean the man couldn't use a bit of intimidation.

On deck, Marcus searched the main deck and forecastle for Gordon as he was a part of the morning watch. The young man was nowhere to be found.

"Good morrow, Captain," Eck said from his position at the tiller. "We should reach our destination within the hour."

Marcus frowned at the knowing smile on his first mate's lips. "What are you smiling about?"

"Why should I not be smiling? It's a bright, clear morning, and I've had a restful night's sleep. You should be smiling too even though I doubt you can say the same about sleep, but then again I'm certain you enjoyed some compensations I did not last night."

"My sleeping habits are not up for discussion."

Eck's smile increased. "Very well, then I'm pleased to inform you the crew are excited to finally arrive at our destination."

"I'm not certain all of them are." Marcus looked about the ship once more. "Where is Gordon?"

Eck tipped his head back, looking skyward. "I sent him aloft to watch for any approaching hazards."

Marcus followed his gaze. "The crow's nest is as good a place to discuss his attempts on Rowena's life as any."

Eck's smile faded. "You think he's responsible for the damage to the sail and locking Rowena in the treasury?"

"Rowena believes so."

"Then approach him cautiously. It's dangerous up there."

Marcus gave a quick nod then moved down the stairs towards the main sail. He gripped the first rope that would take him high above the ship's deck and started climbing. He'd taught his crew to never let go of one rope until you had a hold of another. As he climbed towards the platform atop the main mast, Marcus took his own advice.

When he climbed onto the platform, Gordon startled. "Captain. What brings you up here?"

"We need to discuss why you tried to harm my wife."

Gordon's eyes went wide as he looked about him, knowing he was essentially trapped. "I didn't—"

"Do not lie to me." Marcus's words were harsh and despite the wind they settled between the two of them as thick as any fog.

Gordon's eyes were suddenly blazing. "I dinna think ye remembered such. Yer actions of late say otherwise."

"Because I got married?" Marcus asked in exasperation.

The boat crested a large wave, forcing Gordon to reach for one of the safety lines. "Because yer attention is on her instead of the men who died fer ye, and their families." Steel layered the youthfulness of Gordon's face.

Marcus kept his hands free but widened his stance, riding out the wave. "My commitments have not changed. In fact, by coming to the Cave of Gold, it is my intention to provide the lost crewmen's families with even more compensation." Marcus narrowed his gaze. "Why is what I do for these men's families so important to you?"

"What does it matter?"

Marcus stepped closer. "It matters to me. Why?"

Gordon's fists clenched about the ropes. "Because my brithers, Caley and Mack, both drowned while recoverin' the treasure of Sandwood Bay. I'm all my ma has left."

"And you thought Rowena needed to die for their loss?" Marcus asked, trying to understand.

Gordon glanced away. "A life for a life."

"If you blame anyone for what happened on this ship, it should be me," Marcus said, his voice harsh.

"I should, but I don't," Gordon said with a hint of surprise in his voice. "Ye shared so much of the treasure we did find with the crew. Ye made us all wealthy men." Gordon's lips twisted. "'Twas easier tae hate the woman than tae hate ye."

Marcus released a tense breath. He didn't agree with Gordon's methods, but he could understand his anger over the death of his siblings. Yet even on a ship justice had to be served. "For what you've done, I should lock you in the brig and turn you over to the constable when we next make landfall."

"Nay!" Anger fled and fear brought shadows to Gordon's

eyes. "If somethin' happens tae me, my ma will have no one."

"Perhaps you should have considered that before you attacked my wife." Marcus tried to restrain his irritation. The young man was clearly distressed.

"I dinna kill her."

"You easily could have slain her and others when you sabotaged the sail. Once the line was cut, you had no control of the outcome."

He nodded wearily. "What can I do? How can I make amends?"

"To start, you can return the necklace you stole from me."

Gordon dropped his gaze to his feet. "I'll return it as soon as I'm relieved from duty."

"I'm relieving you from duty right now." Marcus released a heavy sigh. "As the captain of his vessel, I must punish you for what you have done, Gordon. Sabotaging the ship is a serious affair, not to mention endangering my wife. But I am not heartless, nor do I believe you were driven by anything other than your own grief, so I'll allow you to choose either two days and nights in the brig or three lashes. If you choose the brig and if we find the treasure today, I'll have to reduce your share by half since you were not involved in the recovery."

Gordon returned his gaze to Marcus's. "The brig," he said with a look of resignation. "I'm not brave enough tae take the lashings."

"I believe you are, but that is something you will have to learn for yourself. Pain nourishes courage, and loss eventually teaches us to be both brave and wise."

As the two slowly descended to the deck below, Marcus reflected on his own words. Until this moment, he'd only seen the loss of two-and-thirty men as failure on his part. While the loss aboard *The Cliodna* had been tragic, it had also moulded Marcus in ways he hadn't expected. Loss had strengthened his sense of honour and duty, but it had also softened him. He was far more aware of the fragility of life. Tomorrow was guaranteed to no one.

Perhaps that was why he had allowed himself to be persuaded to marry Rowena and why he clung to the idea of her already being with child—to leave some part of himself behind when his days on this earth were through.

AS A GOLDEN light crept through the window of the captain's chamber, Rowena opened her eyes to see Marcus was gone. Disappointment tightened her chest before she forced the emotion away. She'd given Marcus no reason to stay. Besides, he had a ship to run.

After quickly running her fingers through her hair to tame the long locks into some semblance of order before she wove it into a plait, she left the bed, intent to go on deck to get some fresh air. Outside, she moved to the rail on the main deck. She raised her face, drinking in the warmth of the sun and the vigour of the wind.

She'd changed during the past few days. Perhaps it was because of all the obstacles that had been in her path, or perhaps it was because for once she was finally living a life of her own. But today she felt more alive and stronger than she ever had before.

Marcus might also have had something to do with those changes. Only once did she allow her gaze to stray to the forecastle where Marcus stood at the tiller. Just as quickly she pulled her gaze away, turning back to the shoreline slowly coming into view. At peace on this beautiful morning, she closed her eyes and relaxed into the wind.

"You should go back to our cabin and prepare for our arrival. We should disembark within the hour."

She didn't look at Marcus as he settled at the rail beside her. "Why was Gordon trying to harm me?"

Marcus's hands clenched on the railing. "It had little to do with you. He was angry with me over the death of his brothers in our previous treasure hunting. He meant to take his revenge out on me through you. He will be punished."

"Not too harshly, I hope. I was not injured, only frightened."

Marcus was silent a moment. "Gordon returned your necklace to me and is currently in the brig."

Rowena pressed her lips into a thin line at the news. "For

how long?"

"Long enough to contemplate what he's done and realise there are other ways to solve life's problems."

A long moment passed once again with only the wind whispering between them. Rowena felt herself relaxing as she gazed at the blue-green water slipping past. A motion near the wake caught her attention. She smiled when she identified the movement as dark-skinned seals frolicking in and out of the churning water. "I never imagined there would be seals all around Scotland like there are at Dunvegan."

Marcus stared down at the water. "I've never seen them along this part of the coastline. The water is deep and there is nowhere for them to rest out of the water except upon the jagged basalt rocks."

"Do you think they followed us from Dunvegan?"

"It's possible."

"I'm glad they are here. I used to be afraid of them, but no longer. I'd like to think they are a sign of good luck." She sighed into the wind. "I've never been anywhere outside of Dunvegan except to Miss Doddie's School for Girls in Portree. This short voyage has made me realise there is so much more out there waiting to be explored beyond the horizon."

Beside her, he suddenly smiled. "I forget sometimes how beautiful this part of the world is."

"I'm sure other parts of the world are just as wonderful, and filled with exotic things." Excitement flared inside her as she faced him. "I would love to see the pyramids of Egypt or the jungles of Africa."

Marcus raised a brow. "Does Rowena MacLeod have the heart of an explorer?"

"I'd like to think so."

He chuckled and turned to face her with his back at the rail. "Centuries ago, explorers believed that the world was flat, or that dragons awaited beyond the horizon."

"They don't believe that anymore, do they?"

He shook his head. "The discovery of our world continues. European explorers have brought back knowledge about the continents of Africa and the Americas, methods of mapping and navigating have improved with nautical maps, and new foods, plants and animals are being exchanged between the continents." An amused smile lit his face. "The potatoes we eat on this vessel originated in the Americas in a place called Virginia."

"Virginia," she repeated, liking the sound of the foreign land. "You should be proud that you are a part of that explorative tradition."

Sudden anger flashed in his eyes. "I am not an explorer. I'm a treasure hunter and privateer who raids enemy ships for the goods others have gathered from these foreign places."

She tilted her head, considering his sudden change of mood. "You are recovering what was once lost. There is good in that too, Marcus." She reached over and placed a hand on his arm.

He did not shrug her hand away as he turned back to the water. The shoreline was much closer now. Rowena could see the formation of basalt columns. She'd read about the formation of such rocks in one of Orrick's books. The unusual patterns in the rock were left behind when lava cooled on both the upper and lower surfaces, forcing the rock to contract and fracture in a blocky hexagonal pattern.

Rowena gazed upon the rocky shoreline with a sudden mixture of anticipation and dread as a call went out for all hands on deck. Men raced to their stations at the sails and near the anchor, preparing to bring the ship to a stop.

Marcus pushed away from the railing. "Since you want to be an explorer, prepare yourself to come with me and a few others as we make our first exploratory run at the cave."

She smothered a smile. "You want me with you?"

He nodded. "How else can I be certain nothing happens to you while I am off the ship? It will be perfectly safe. No one will be leaving the boat. We need to check the tide, measure the depth of the water, and the strength of the currents before we explore the cave on foot. Not only is the cave hard to find, it's also a dangerous place, which is why no one comes here."

"Why do you think our ancestors called it the Cave of Gold long before Jacob Thorne stored his treasure there?"

"Most likely because of the yellow lichens that cover the rock formations. Or perhaps it is the glow of the setting sun on the rocks at the cave's entrance that turns them to gold. Either way, I am certain the sea cave will reveal all its secrets to us very soon." He straightened, glancing at the men running across the deck. "I must return to my duty."

She nodded, watching Marcus take the steps up to the forecastle two at a time. Some of the men on deck scrambled up the masts to gather up the sails while others moved to drop the anchor.

Allowing her thoughts to drift, Rowena gazed back to the shoreline where a dark opening appeared in the side of the westward-facing cliff. A strong sense of premonition made her skin tingle. Was it a warning that perhaps they weren't meant to be here, that the cave was not ready to give up her treasure to them?

Rowena swallowed against the sudden tightness in her throat as she remembered the stories she'd heard about this mystical place; that it extended to Fairyland or as far as Hell; that a ferocious green dog guarded it, ready to kill whoever entered its den. But it was the last myth that sent her heartbeat thudding in her chest. It claimed that no one who had entered the cave had ever come out.

Surely that wasn't correct if Jacob Thorne had placed his looted treasures deep within the cave. Rowena released a tense breath. Either way, she and Marcus were about to learn the truth about the Cave of Gold when they ventured into its depth together.

CHAPTER FIFTEEN

ROWENA CLUTCHED THE sides of the boat as Marcus steered them into the narrow mouth of the cave. Bryce, Rob Roy, Mack, and Naill were all silent as they held their lanterns aloft, lighting the way. Though it was daylight outside, there was no light inside the cave other than what they brought with them.

The walls glistened with moisture, and an earthy, musty scent pervaded the air as they slowly progressed inside. Beneath them the water was clear, exposing a rocky floor that appeared deeper than Rowena was tall. Even the men might not be able to walk upon the cave's bottom with their heads above water. It was hard to judge anything in this enclosed space that seemed as though it was from another world instead of their own.

The boat barely passed through the opening, scraping here and there on the rock formations as they moved silently past. Rob Roy held his lantern high, searching the shadows. After a long moment he relaxed his arm and swung back to the others. "'Tis pleased I am that nae giant green dog was 'ere tae greet us, devour us, or drag us tae Hell."

"Amen to that," Mack agreed, though his face remained tense as he searched the darkness ahead. "Do ye hear somethin'?"

The only sounds that came to Rowena's ears were the dipping of the oars into the water and the swishing of the boat as it glided forward.

Rob Roy sat straighter on the wooden seat. "It sounds like the skirl of a bag pipe deep within the cave." His face turned ashen. "'Tis warning us tae not go any farther."

"What are you talking about?" Bryce squinted in the darkness beyond this lantern. "There's nothing but silence."

"Nay," Rob Roy objected. "I hear a piper. The sound is coming from either Fairyland or Hell." He stood up, rocking the boat from side to side. "We have tae turn around. Go back."

"Sit down." Marcus's authoritative voice cut through the man's fears.

His gaze shifted to Marcus and colour came back to his cheeks a heartbeat before he returned to his seat.

"There is nothing to fear in this cave, Rob Roy. I won't let anything happen to any of you. Besides, this is an explorative mission that will help us decide what tools we bring with us to explore the cave further. Only a few more moments and we will turn around. I promise."

Marcus's words seemed to ease the tension that had overcome the men in the boat, but Rowena knew there were things even Marcus couldn't control. She tightened her grip on the side of the boat at the sensation of the earth trembling around them. The water alongside the boat rippled. The impressions were faint and no one else in the boat seemed to notice, but she had. Then as quick as it came, the trembling stopped. Rowena pressed her lips together, deciding not to say anything that might unsettle Rob Roy any more than he already was.

Silence pervaded the cave as they drifted forward until the boat came to a jarring stop. The sound of wood grating on rock echoed around them as they each scrambled to keep their seats.

"We hit a rock shelf," Marcus said, standing and searching the path before them with his lantern. He stepped from the boat onto the rock and disappeared into the distance for several long moments before he returned with something in his hand.

At the boat's edge, he handed something shiny to Bryce, who held it up, revealing a golden goblet. "There was only the one piece lying on the rock in the short distance I explored, but it is proof enough that the treasure is here."

Bryce jumped from the boat with his lantern and disappeared into the darkness.

Marcus turned to the other men in the boat. "This was not meant to be a retrieval mission, so I will leave it up to the three of you, do you wish to keep exploring, or do you wish to go back and send others to recover the treasure?"

Rob Roy, Mack, and Naill shared tense glances before

Naill finally replied, "We'll stay to help take back what we can of the treasure. No sense sendin' another boat when we are already here."

The men stepped over the sides of the boat and followed Bryce deeper into the cave. When they were out, Marcus dragged the boat farther onto the rock shelf to make certain it would not dislodge before they were ready, then he offered Rowena his hand. "It is safe enough for you to explore, if you are up to it."

She accepted his hand and allowed him to help her out of the boat. Together they followed the others. As they walked farther back, Rowena looked around at the basalt pillars that made up the sides of the cave, running as high as the roof of a cathedral, deep into the rock that had been eternally swept by a deep and swelling sea.

Rowena stopped. "Is it safe to go back there?"

Marcus came to her side and took her hand in his. "There are risks, but let us pray it will be fine. Exploring on foot is safer than diving deep in the water with the waves endlessly trying to dash you against the rocks as you retrieve treasure." He gave her hand a squeeze as excitement filled his eyes. "Come with me."

With a deep shuddering breath, Rowena shoved her fear aside and put her trust in Marcus. The lanterns created myriad twisting, dancing lights. Golden hues sent the shadows writhing before them into the deeper recesses of the cave. The earthy scent of ancient dirt and wet rocks surrounded them as they kept walking hand in hand. Darkness pressed in on her. She couldn't see anything but the light-wreathed silhouette of Marcus's body. The temperature in the cave dropped and she wrapped her free hand about her waist in an effort to keep warm.

The shuffling of their footsteps mingled with the quickened puffs of their breathing as they continued. After another fifty feet or so, light from the other lanterns merged with their own. They continued forward, and when the light touched two treasure chests filled with silver and gold, Rowena's breath jammed in her throat. "The treasure is real." The words bounced off the walls and rang back at her.

Bryce turned to greet them. Excitement brightened his eyes. "I'm sorry for every bad thing I ever did to you or said to you, Cousin. You too, Rowena." He turned back to the chest before him. "The treasure is smaller than I imagined it would be, but that matters not. It is still an amazing find."

"This isn't all of it, not according to what Jacob Thorne told me anyway. There has to be more farther back in the cave."

Excitement pounded in Rowena's chest as she stared not only at the treasure but also at the men who had previously been so uncertain and were now smiling and laughing, running metallic coins through their fingers. Their fears had vanished in a haze of silver and gold.

"Shall we keep going deeper into the cave?" Bryce asked, his voice animated.

Marcus shook his head. "Let's focus on getting these two chests loaded onto the boat. Then Rob Roy, Naill, and Mack can take them back to the ship and send others to gather more. The treasure will take up all the extra space in the small vessel so there won't be enough room for all of us to return. Therefore, you, Rowena, and I will keep exploring."

Rowena shivered. Staying behind in the darkness of the cave unnerved her even though Marcus would be with her.

The men dragged the chests to the boat, then Marcus and Bryce pushed the laden boat fully into the water once more. The three who would stay behind watched as the lanterns on the boat slowly faded from sight. When silence wrapped around them, Marcus turned to Bryce. "Do you want to take the lead or should I?"

"You would allow that?"

Marcus handed one of the two remaining lanterns to his cousin. "This treasure hunt was what you wanted. Go forward and earn your portion."

Bryce headed for the ever-narrowing passageway ahead of them.

Marcus once more took her hand and followed. As they moved along the passageway, the ground beneath them dipped down. A stream of water covered the rock, but a bank was visible again on the opposite side. Marcus released Rowena's hand and jumped across. "Come. It's a fairly easy crossing. Worst that will happen is your boots might get wet."

Her heart sped up, and a tumbling mix of excitement and anxiety dampened her palms, turning them cold and clammy. With a leap, she made it easily to the other side. They continued walking. Only the sound of their breathing and their soft footfalls echoed around them. The cold dampness of the stone walls seeped into Rowena's bones and plastered her leather tunic and trousers to her skin, but she didn't notice the discomfort. All she could think about was the treasure that may lie ahead and how it would fund her future life.

After what felt like an eternity, Bryce stopped.

"What is it?" Marcus asked.

"There are two tunnels. Which direction should we head?" As Bryce held his lantern aloft it wobbled in his hands, causing the light to vibrate haphazardly across the arched entrances to two tunnels.

"It should be safe enough for us to split up. Since it will take a while for the men to return from the ship, we have time to explore. What do you say we each progress deeper into the cave for five hundred paces, then head back here to report?"

Bryce shrugged. "Fine by me as long as you take Rowena with you."

"Of course." Marcus took her hand, and they moved towards the tunnel on the left.

"I'm betting the treasure is this way." With a grin, Bryce headed for the tunnel on the right.

Deep inside the tunnel Rowena remained quiet, not wanting to interrupt Marcus's counting of his paces, but she couldn't stop thinking about the earlier trembling she'd experienced. Marcus did not seem to notice, nor did he seem to feel the uneasiness she was feeling.

When Marcus reached five hundred paces, he stopped. They'd come to a larger opening in the tunnel. On one side, the rock dipped downward. On the other, there was a kind of platform. Marcus released her hand and jumped onto the elevated rock, searching the shadows. It would have been a perfect place to store more of the treasure. "Hmm," he said, turning back towards her and jumping down. "Nothing is here." He held the lantern higher, illuminating the distance.

"What if we can't find any more of Jacob Thorne's treasure?"

"Then we've lost nothing. What we did find will be enough for the men and Bryce to live well for what remains of their lifetimes."

"Yet you wanted more for your men."

Marcus shrugged. "No amount of treasure will ever assuage the guilt I feel over their loss."

"Oh, Marcus, before anyone else can forgive you, you must forgive yourself. What happened was not your fault." She had meant to say more but a sudden odd sound in the distance stopped her. Marcus must have heard it too by the expression on his face. "What is that?"

He didn't answer as they both kept listening to the

shushing sound growing ever louder and closer. Suddenly water swirled into the tunnel where they stood, covering their feet in the span of a heartbeat, with more rushing in.

"Come with me, Rowena, quickly." Marcus moved to the elevated rock. "Give me your hand." After jumping onto the platform, he stretched his hand down and lifted her up. His hands came about her waist as he pulled her back from the ledge. In a matter of moments, the entire chamber was filled with rushing water.

"What is happening?" Rowena asked, turning to Marcus. At the look on his face, fear clutched her.

"The tide. How could I have been so foolish as to forget about the tide?" Agony reverberated in his tone.

Despite her fear she would not allow him to add this burden to those he already carried. "Tides come in and go. All we have to do is wait it out. This shelf seems to have protected us from the water. In six hours the water should recede and we will be able to make our way back to your men, who will no doubt be waiting for us."

"And if this is just the beginning of the higher tide, then we might possibly drown in the next six hours." He ran his fingers through his hair. "'Tis my worst nightmare coming true all over again."

Rowena drew a breath and released it, trying to remain calm. Giving in to terror would not help either of them in this situation. "I am going to believe that this will be the worst of it. Come." She motioned back towards where he'd set the lantern. "Let's sit and conserve our strength for the journey out of here in six hours."

He hesitated. "What about Bryce?"

"He's clever and resourceful, as all MacDonalds seem to be." Rowena smiled. "He'll find a way just as we did to wait this out."

Marcus released a deep shuddering breath before joining her near the lantern. They both sat down. "You are right about one thing. All we can do is wait." He turned to look at the candle in the lantern. "We only have about four hours of light left. If we are going to make certain we can avoid any dangers on our way back out of this cavern, then we'll have to extinguish the light."

Rowena swallowed roughly. She wasn't afraid of the dark and Marcus was with her, but willingly pitching themselves into total darkness while they couldn't see whether the water was rising or receding left her unsettled. Yet it was something that had to be done. "You can relight the wick?"

He patted his sporran. "I have flint and steel."

Rowena looked about her. There was nothing they could use in the cave to make a fire. "Very well."

"Take a good look around. Try to memorise our little shelf in case we need to move about."

She did, and when she could look no more she finally nodded.

At her signal, Marcus opened the lantern and extinguished the light until darkness unlike anything she'd ever known surrounded them.

"It's all right, Rowena." Marcus reached for her hand. His voice seemed disembodied, yet she could feel him right beside her and took comfort in that. The sound of rushing water had slowed. The lapping of the water against the edge of their safe haven wrapped around them. Only a hand's width separated her from Marcus and she could sense every action of his body. The rise and fall of his chest as he breathed, the tension of his hands as he ran them across his breeches.

The scent of the earth and the salt water from the sea mixed with the warm, clean male fragrance that belonged to Marcus. She wanted to breathe in the aroma, take it into her nostrils, into her body. The thought sent a ripple of shocked awareness through her. That suddenly wasn't all of him she wanted in her body. She wanted to be joined with him in the same searing fashion that she had known last night. She could not see him, but she could touch every part of him while they waited for whatever might happen next in this dark and dangerous cave.

She moistened her lips with her tongue and reached for Marcus. For a heartbeat she hesitated. What about the possibility of a bairn? Rowena's hand hung suspended partway between her body and Marcus's. If she were already pregnant, then another joining would hardly matter. If she were not, then their lovemaking could expose her to further risk.

She pulled her fingers back, sitting with the indecision in her chest. Her body burned even as her mind spun through every scenario, until she finally decided that in their present situation there was no guarantee of a tomorrow. Only the here and now mattered. She hoped Marcus would feel the same way as she once again extended her hand until it made contact with his muscular arm. She shifted closer and ran her fingers over his sculpted flesh. She'd never felt so powerful, or so terrified of both death and his refusal.

"What are you doing?" His voice was deep and gravelled in the silence of the cave.

Now that she'd made her decision, confidence filled her. "I need something to take my mind off our present situation." She wished she could see what was in his eyes.

He must have had the same thought because she heard him fumbling around in this sporran, no doubt searching for his flint and steel.

"Don't light the lantern," she said, finding his hand and stilling his movements. "I don't want to see how far the water has risen. I'd like to continue to believe we are safe enough for now."

He took her hand in his. "I can understand that. It is difficult sitting here and thinking that at any moment we might drown." He paused. "Are you certain you wish to pass the time in such an intimate way?" His voice was thick, laced with intensity.

She squeezed his hand before releasing it, finding his torso and feathering her hands up his chest. "I want only to feel. To not think about anything except the pleasure we can bring each other. If we are to face death, I want to feel desired, cared for . . ." *Loved.* Rowena bit her lip to stop the word. But it was true. She was in love with Marcus. This Marcus, not the one from her past. The realisation crashed over her with the power of a rogue wave. And he was going to hurt her. Not today when they shared this moment, but when he left her at Dunvegan after their marriage was annulled. After that, he would move on to settle his debts without her. She wanted all of him, today and forever. But that was impossible. Once their marriage was over, he would never allow her on his ship again.

So, she would settle for this moment. The beauty of loving him in this moment would dull the edges of the knife that would eventually cut into her heart. "I need you, Marcus. I want you."

Marcus exhaled in a whoosh of air. "We came on this adventure to help erase my sins, to find treasure to placate the families of those whose lives I destroyed, and yet I am the one receiving a priceless treasure." He pulled his shirt out from where it was tucked into his breeches and began unbuttoning it. When he was done, he spread his shirt on the rock, creating a layer of warmth and dryness. "I swore I would never take that treasure unless you gifted it to me."

"I am offering myself to you." Her fingers found the silken flesh that had been beneath his shirt. Thick muscles flexed as she ran her fingers over his chest where it separated into eight defined ridges of hard flesh. She remembered from last night that his nipples were dark, flat disks in a wide chest sprinkled with black hair, and that his hair was thicker below his belly button, creating a trail disappearing into his breeches.

With a groan of impatience, she reached for the ties of his breeches. His hand snaked out to stop her. "If you touch me there at this moment, you will undo me before we even get started."

Did she truly have that much power over him? "I do not mean to force you into anything, Marcus. If you do not want me . . ."

Marcus growled in frustration and tightened his grip. "Not want you? How could any man not want you? You are all I want. My body aches for you, but I can't give you what you deserve. Don't you see that?"

"In this moment, none of that matters, Marcus. It is simply you and me. Nothing else exists."

CHAPTER SIXTEEN

O VER THE PAST six months on his ship, Marcus had seen how a grey day could be brightened by a fleeting moment of light as the sun found a break in the clouds while dropping to the horizon. He'd also seen the purple, gold, and green lights of the *Na Fir-Chlis* "dance" with the stars against the blackness of night. So many days and nights had stolen his breath with their beauty, their magnificence, but he'd never imagined anything more exquisite than the sound of Rowena's voice asking him to merge his body with hers.

How he wanted to light the lantern so he could see her face as he touched her for what would most likely be the last time. Death or distance could keep them apart in the future. Marcus blew out a shaky breath. "You are right. All we have is now. Let us not waste a moment."

He could hear Rowena moving. "Since I cannot see you, tell me what you are doing."

She sucked in a breath. "I am releasing my hair from its plait."

"Would you allow me?" He reached out his hands and once he found her shoulders, he ran his fingers up her neck to her jawline then around to where her hair was secured by a tie. He loosened the tie and gently allowed his fingers to slide through her heavy hair, tugging the plait until her long locks flowed freely. He brought the ends to his nose and drew in her scent. "Your hair smells like sunshine and heather. It has always reminded me of home." He settled the long waves over her shoulders and ran his hands down her arms before moving back up until he found the laces on her tunic.

"May I remove your clothes?"

"Aye." The word was a plea.

Last night he had looked his fill at her naked body. He pulled that memory into his thoughts as he slowly unlaced her tunic, opening it and slowly sliding it over her shoulders and from her arms. He quickly unlaced her stays, exposing her upper body to the cool air in the cave, and yet her skin was warm where he touched.

"Now I'll be removing your boots, trousers, and drawers." She reclined on the shirt he'd spread out earlier, allowing him to first remove her boots and hose before exploring her long, lean muscles as he released her legs from their leather coverings. Rowena's body was slim and yet also muscular. Her stomach was tight, her legs long and shapely. Her body was sleek and powerful and perfect. He'd seen one light scar upon her flesh, at the top of her right knee, where she'd told him she'd fallen down the hard stone stairway at the front entrance of Dunvegan as a child. She'd had no mother to patch up her wound, and instead of telling her brothers of her injury, she'd hidden it away, not wanting to appear weak in front of a household of men. Marcus bent forward and pressed a kiss to the resulting scar.

Her breath hitched.

If he could see her, he knew she would be frowning. Rowena saw her scar as a flaw. He saw it as a sign of strength, the sign of a survivor.

"Now that you've undressed me, it's my turn to finish undressing you." Hungrily, she reached for his waist and untied his breeches. Pushing the fabric aside, his manhood sprang forward, hard and pulsing as it met the cool cavern air. Rowena left his breeches, to quickly remove his boots and stockings. When she was done, she pressed her mouth against his in a kiss that tasted of desperation and desire. She pulled away and quickly divested him of his breeches until they were both naked in the darkness. He reached for the garments they'd removed, setting them around his shirt, making a nest for them atop the rock.

He leaned forward and captured her lips, licking the seam and tasting her depths as she opened to him. He pressed his warm body against hers and pulled her down, stretching his body next to hers.

"I want to touch you. May I?" she asked.

"You can do whatever you want." Marcus put both hands behind his head to stop from taking control of the moment. If she needed to learn his body, he would give her that time. He clenched his jaw against the sweet torture of her fingers feathering over his skin. She sat up, running her hands over his shoulders, down his chest. She circled his nipples with her thumbs, and he groaned, closing his eyes and revelling in the pressure. When her soft touch was replaced with wet heat, his breath caught.

She moved her explorations lower, and Marcus tried to think of anything but her breath tickling his hair, her hands bumping over his stomach muscles as she moved closer to his throbbing manhood.

When she wrapped her strong fingers around his erect member, her exhalation of awe washed across his over-sensitised skin, and Marcus wondered if he could die from pleasure as she stroked him tentatively.

"Does it feel good when I do this?"

"Yes." Marcus shuddered. "I like it too much. You'd better stop." He shifted their bodies until she was beneath him. "Last night I wanted you so badly I took more than I gave. This time, it will be different." He ran his fingers over her body, hoping that he left a trail of fire across her breasts, her throat, her belly. His hands nudged her legs apart and he moved between them, stroking the nest of curls surrounding her womanhood. His fingers splayed out to tangle and play. After a while, he bent down and slowly rubbed his cheek against her curls. The faint abrasion of her curls was wildly exciting. He nipped gently at her softness and then his tongue followed to soothe and tease. Her muscles tightened, but he brought up his hand to her belly to relax her. "You wanted to forget about everything. Relax. Give in to the sensations and let them take you where they will."

"Relax? Every muscle inside me is vibrating in anticipation."

He laughed and the sound echoed through the darkness. "Wrong word, forgive me. Allow yourself to melt. Let me help you in that endeavour."

He trailed his fingers across her mons and then explored farther down until he found what he was looking for, and began to press, rotate, and flick.

She gave a low cry and her fingers clenched helplessly in his hair. When he plunged two fingers inside her wetness, she groaned, and he could hear what he thought was her head moving back and forth as he began a rhythm that sent her into convulsions of pleasure and hunger.

"Marcus!"

"Hush, my sweet. Let me pleasure you for a while. It will make the rest so much better." He wanted to pleasure her with an intensity that surprised him. Her every response was linked in some mysterious fashion to his own. Every taut muscle of hers communicated her pleasure and that same sensation echoed within him.

Marcus continued his pulsing rhythm inside her as he shifted his body upwards to suck a ripe nipple into his mouth, swirling his tongue over the rigid flesh. Rowena cried out again, but he gave her no mercy. He nipped, licked, and suckled one breast, before moving to the other. Her body tightened beneath him. Slowly, he pushed his finger deeper into her cleft, feeling her intimate muscles clench.

Last night their lovemaking had been fast and furious, two bodies that had long been denied the pleasure they'd both longed for. Today, he wanted to stretch things out. To show her as much pleasure as he could so that when they parted they would each have their memories of this moment to hold on to. He explored her body with desperation, communicating to her his hunger, his need.

ROWENA WAS FALLING into a pool of sensation, and she longed to tumble further still, now that he had invited her into this world of delight and bliss. Marcus's mouth was hot and insistent on her breast. His finger pressed deeper into her, burning sweetly as her body tightened around him.

Rowena arched her body. When he released her breasts, she wrapped her legs around his hips. Her core was empty and aching. She pulled him closer to the most intimate part of herself, the steel ridge of his erection nudging her wet, slick flesh. She rubbed against him. "I need you, Marcus, now."

Awaiting no further invitation, he entered her, slowly, letting her become accustomed to his fullness. He began to move, alternating short strokes with long ones. He would move swiftly, then with infinite slowness, until the sound of their mingled breath echoed around them. If death were imminent, this would be the way to go, cocooned in a sea of pleasure.

Needing more of him, Rowena raised her hips, undulating her lower body to try to hold him inside her a heartbeat longer. At his gasp of ecstasy, she repeated the movement, realising she could give him the same gratification he gave her.

"Merciful heavens." Marcus's body grew more taut with each movement of her hips. "You're making me lose control."

"Relax into the sensations," she breathed, repeating his own advice.

His breath was coming in rough gasps as he plunged deep. "I'm taking you over the edge of glory with me." He cupped her bottom, holding her still as his strokes became hard and hot, searing her in a fever of heated pleasure. She felt something building, tightening deep within her.

"Rowena—" The word was a ragged plea and a prayer as the tension inside her that had been building shattered in a wondrous rapture, shaking her to the depths of her soul. She clenched around Marcus and heard his low cry above her as he joined her in endless glory.

Rowena relaxed back into the clothing beneath them, filled with a satisfaction she had never known. "When we catch our breath, can we do that again?"

Marcus's chest rumbled with laughter as he lifted off her and settled next to her, pulling her into his arms until her head rested on his shoulder. "We can do that as many times as you wish, but I think it's best if we rest for a while."

A surge of emotion swelled inside her. She nestled her cheek against his shoulder, her hand drifting over the solid wall of his chest in a slow, sleepy caress even as a stab of sorrow pierced the haze of their lovemaking. What would she ever do without him in her life? As quickly as it had come, she forced the thought away. Now was not the time to walk that road. At this moment, he was hers and she was his. That was all she would think about.

Marcus remained silent for a long while. Rowena was half-certain he had fallen asleep when he kissed the top of her head and said, "Rowena, I need to turn the lamp on for just a moment to check on the water."

Despite the languidness that had stolen over her body, she stiffened at the thought of finding the water had risen even higher towards their safe platform. She sat up and Marcus did the same, reaching no doubt for his sporran and the flint and steel inside.

In the next moment, light flared. At first it was so bright she had to turn away from it, until her eyes adjusted. Once they did, she turned back towards the edge of the platform and released her breath in a rush. The water was no higher than before. In fact, it looked like it had receded ever so slightly. "Are we safe?" she asked hopefully.

"Not until the water recedes fully, but that prospect is growing more favourable with every passing moment." He turned to her and smiled. Her chest tightened at the tenderness in his gaze as it passed over her body. "You are truly beautiful, Rowena MacLeod."

She swallowed roughly, wanting to correct him. She was in every sense of the law a MacDonald, but she held herself in check. "You, Marcus, are everything a woman could ever want in a man. You are strong, yet also tender and loving." In the golden light she studied him, trying to memorise the curves and lines of his body. This might be her last chance to see him naked. She would make that moment count.

His smile slipped as he stared at her for a heartbeat, then turned back to the lantern. "I should blow this out. We still need to conserve what candle wax we have left in order to find our way out of here."

The world around them faded into velvet blackness once more. He set the lantern aside and shuffled back towards her. To her surprise, he settled beside her once more and pulled her tight against the wall of his chest. "Try to rest. It will still be a while until the water recedes."

Rowena tried to sleep, but that forgetful state would not come. She was drowsy and her body was replete with satisfaction. Even so, deep inside, a lingering fear refused to go away. How long would this moment with Marcus last—a few more hours, perhaps a few more days?

She stared into the darkness, embracing the man in her

arms. The water was receding. For however long that took, the dream of a loving husband who wanted her by his side would be a reality. They had been given a gift in this cavern, beyond time and place, where they could be lovers. Where she could pretend that the long, slow caresses and rich drugging kisses Marcus offered meant more than they did.

It was much easier in the darkness to show Marcus how much she cared about him through lingering kisses and intimate caresses. To show him what he meant to her that was still difficult to articulate in the light of day. To ignore risk and future plans.

To simply love him.

She pressed a kiss to his chest and snuggled deeper into his arms. She closed her eyes as love welled and poured through her. Sated, replete, and deeply satisfied, she surrendered to the darkness even as her lips silently mouthed a prayer. They needed a miracle to happen, and soon, if they were to have any sort of future at all.

CHAPTER SEVENTEEN

ARCUS LISTENED TO the slow, even sound of Rowena's breathing as he stared out into the suffocating darkness. If she weren't by his side, he would be terrified of the nothingness that stretched all around them. He tightened his arms around Rowena until the beat of her heart could be felt against his own. Yearning and tenderness unlike anything he'd ever known filled him.

He should not have taken what Rowena offered him, but he could not have stopped himself. The discovery of what she meant to him had shattered his control and torn aside the veil he had used to mask the truth even from himself. And now that they had shared their love again, he knew he would never be able to let her go. The love he felt in her every touch was even more compelling an argument for them to stay together than his guilt.

He had to find a way to make things right with both Rowena and the families of his men. This treasure was supposed to help Rowena fund a life of her own, without him. But he no longer wanted such a thing. He wanted her beside him every day and every night from this moment forward.

Marcus stared unseeingly into the darkness, turning over in his mind every possible way for him to remain with Rowena and yet still fulfil his duty to the families of the men he'd lost. Perhaps they should end their hunt for the remaining treasure. What they'd already found would keep everyone in a state of comfort for the rest of their lives.

A frown tugged at Marcus's lips. He'd also exposed the location of Jacob Thorne's treasure to every man on *The Cliodna*, to Bryce, and to Rowena. Had Bryce already found the treasure in the tunnel he had chosen? If not, would any of them return to *Uamh Oir* to retrieve what they might have failed to fully find during this attempt? Did he care that Jacob's treasure was now exposed?

Marcus pressed his lips together. He didn't care about the treasure itself. He did care about the lives that might be lost if anyone alone tried to retrieve the treasure.

God's blood. They had come this far. Perhaps he should see the entire search through to either prove that nothing else existed deep in these caves, or that it did.

Alternatives skittered through his thoughts. *Don't think, not of tomorrow.* His fingers reached out to sculpt Rowena's body, reverently, possessively, still not quite believing that she was his.

She moved beneath his caress, sensuously, taking her time to let the pleasure of their lovemaking sink into her core. She cried out with satisfaction as he moved over her, parted her legs with his hard muscled thighs and with one powerful thrust, filled her. She arched beneath him and cried out again as passion crested quickly, breaking over them both in a long, glorious wave of ecstasy.

Holding the moment and each other they settled against their soft cocoon. Marcus pulled Rowena close as they both sank into slumber. He would solve all his problems when next he woke. Until then, he would cherish the woman in his arms as if they were the only two people left in this world.

———— ∿∿ ————

ROWENA WOKE SUDDENLY and stared into the darkness. It was difficult to tell how much time had passed. Had she been asleep only minutes or had hours gone by? Even if they lit the lantern one more time, they would not be able to tell. Yet she knew even without the light that something was different.

A sound echoed through the cave.

She sat up, listening, but only silence settled around her and Marcus. Perhaps it was only wishful thinking. With a sigh, she ran her fingers over their clothing, trying to locate her stays. It took a while but she finally located something both soft and stiff. Pulling the garment free from its position just under Marcus's right elbow, she wrapped it around her chest and started the arduous process of lacing the garment up without the aid of sight.

The echo came to her again. This time it sounded closer.

"Marcus." Rowena shook his shoulder, trying to wake him. She could feel him bolt upright beside her, as though he'd forgotten where they were. "I heard an unusual sound."

They both remained silent, listening. After several long moments the sound came again.

Marcus fumbled around in the darkness for a heartbeat before she heard a scratching sound and light flooded the chamber. It took a moment before Rowena could see as her eyes adjusted to the brightness. When she could, she looked to Marcus. "What do you think it is?"

He stood and moved to the edge of the platform. "The water has receded. Perhaps it is the men coming to find us." He turned and strode back to her. "Dress quickly. We don't want to waste a moment."

Rowena sorted through the pile for her clothing before looking down at her stays. She chuckled at the terrible job she'd done finding the brackets to lace the garment closed. Even so, the haphazard lacing would have to do for now. Wasting no time, she finished dressing, grateful for the light. She was thrilled to be free of the trap the water had created, but also saddened by the end of this precious time alone with Marcus.

When they were both dressed, Marcus picked up the lantern and jumped down from the ledge before offering her his hand. When she was beside him, his gaze washed over her and he smiled. "As strange as it sounds, I'm glad we had this time together." He squeezed her hand.

"Me too." She returned his smile though inside her heart constricted a little. He took her arm, wound it with his and they set off. They had only gone a few paces before another lantern's light spilled into their private retreat.

Bryce and two other men came forward. Yellow-gold light spilled through the chamber, illuminating the stark basalt walls. "Praise heaven you are alive," Bryce said as his gaze passed between the two of them.

"We're glad to see you. Did you get trapped by the tide?" Marcus asked.

Bryce nodded. "Not nearly as deep into the cave as you. The tunnel I went into moved upwards whereas yours went down. After going five hundred paces, I made my way back as we'd agreed. I made it all the way back to where the cave split into two before I became trapped." Bryce tilted his head towards the two men who had accompanied him. "When Rob Roy and Mack returned with two boats, we all decided to come looking for you and Rowena."

Rowena removed her arm from Marcus's and stepped back, letting the men continue to talk. She took the lantern from Marcus's hand and walked around the cave, exploring the odd formations that made up the walls.

"Did you find treasure in here?" Bryce asked.

"Nay," Marcus replied.

A smile came to Bryce's lips. "I found two chests filled with silver and gold coins in the tunnel I followed. The chests are already loaded on the boats."

"That leaves ten more treasure chests if what Jacob Thorne told me was true. We did not have time to explore this branch of the cave for long before the water rushed in, trapping us on a ledge back there."

Rowena let the men's conversation flow over her as she continued studying the rocks. Reaching out, she trailed her fingers over the rough surface. She'd never seen such patterns as these before. These rocks had been here long before she had ever lived and would be here long after she died. Now that fear had passed, she was able to truly see the magnificence of the stone before her. In awe, she allowed her fingers to continue their exploration until suddenly there was nothing beneath them.

Bringing the lantern up, she peered at the gap before her. The opening had not been visible to them when they'd entered, because the rocks before her overlapped, making the wall seem solid when it was not. Even so, the gap in the rocks was not large, there was barely enough space for her to slip her shoulders into the gap. It took a moment to wiggle her hips through, but when she did, she held up the lantern to reveal another long tunnel.

Rowena stepped farther into the tunnel, and the voices behind her drifted away. She walked down the tunnel quite a ways when suddenly she stopped. There in the middle of the tunnel sat ten chests loaded with silver bullion, spices, gold, pearls, and emeralds.

Rowena gazed spellbound, barely breathing at the sight before her. She'd found the remaining treasure. Gold and silver coins were spilled all over the cave floor, indicating that the tide came in this far to wash over the treasure on a regular basis. Many items were still contained in their chests. She moved to examine them, counting four chests filled to overflowing with gold bullion and pearls, three chests with black-encrusted bricks that could only be silver bullion, and green-encrusted jewels, and three more chests with clay jars covered in algae.

From the top of one of the chests, Rowena retrieved a leather pouch and untied the fastening wrapped around the opening. Inside she saw large, creamy-coloured pearls that had once been a long necklace as evidenced by the fragment of silk thread that remained. She loosened her tunic and stuffed the leather pouch inside before closing her tunic once more. The small treasure had barely settled against the inside of her fairy armour when a roar from the very bowels of the earth echoed all around her. The rocky floor beneath her feet rippled and swayed as if it were alive, forcing her to stagger.

"An earthquake." The panic in her voice bounced off the narrow walls. Rocks showered all around her as she retreated, forcing her to zigzag her steps to avoid being struck. Nervously she tightened her grip on the lantern and pushed forward. She'd felt tremors like this in the earth before. Their steward, Becks, used to tell her and her brothers such trembling was caused by the tension between earth and water.

"I'm surrounded by both earth and water." The rumbling continued as Rowena staggered back to the gap. It was just ahead. She should have paid more attention to the trembling she'd felt earlier. The cave had tried to warn them that something terrible would happen, but neither she nor Marcus had listened to the subtle signals from the earth.

Only a few more steps . . . An ear-shattering grinding sounded. Several large stones broke away from the ceiling, falling to partially block her exit. She could still scramble over the tops if she hurried. More rocks rained down. Rowena surged forward. Her breath came in spurts as her heart pounded in her ears. She reached the gap, but skidded to a stop when three large boulders fell, blocking her path. "Nay!" she cried as terror wormed its icy, insidious tentacles through her body.

Why had she gone off by herself? Rowena dropped to her knees. Smaller rocks continued to pelt her body, but the fairy armour seemed impenetrable as each rock bounced off, neither piercing the leather nor bruising the flesh beneath. Then, as quickly as it had begun, the earth stopped shaking. An oppressive silence surrounded her.

This time she was stranded in a cave alone. "Marcus!" She screamed his name, praying he would somehow hear her. The word vibrated in the chamber for a long moment, then disappeared. Beside her, the light in the lantern sputtered before it caught more fully again.

Rowena clung to the lantern's handle. What had Marcus said earlier? That there was only enough candle left for about four hours of light? *Four hours.* With great effort, she drew a calming breath and set the lantern aside. That meant she had four hours to try and push some of the rocks away so she could escape the all-consuming darkness and the tide that would rise once more in a matter of hours.

CHAPTER EIGHTEEN

A S THE WORLD around them began to shake, Marcus turned and looked back at where he'd last seen Rowena. His heart stopped when she was nowhere in sight.

"Rowena?" He raced towards the wall where he'd last noticed her presence.

"She was just here," Bryce said, coming to join his cousin, holding the lantern high. Rob Roy and Mack followed behind them, their lanterns swaying with the undulating bed of the cave, causing the light to spill across in a twisting, contorting fashion.

Sounds both earthy and unearthly reverberated through the cave as chunks of rock crumbled from the ceiling, forcing the men to slow their progress. When they finally made it to the wall of the cave, they moved slowly along the edge as Marcus had last seen Rowena do. "There has to be something here that we are missing."

"Are ye sure 'tis safe to remain in the cave?" Mack asked. "What if the ceilin' comes down on our heads?"

Marcus ground his teeth. He was uncertain of anything other than his need to find Rowena. "If you'd feel safer out of the tunnel, then go ahead. I won't stop you."

Both men looked at each other for a heartbeat before shaking their heads. "Ye've been beside us durin' all our troubles. We won't abandon ye now."

"As long as that is your choice," Marcus replied. He would never forgive himself if these brave men died in this earthquake. He'd already lost too many of his crew needlessly.

"It is," Rob Roy said, his voice determined. "The sooner we find the missus, the sooner we can all leave."

"Agreed." Marcus turned back to the stone, feeling each ridge and valley in the oddly shaped formations. Rob Roy and Mack moved several paces ahead and studied the wall as Marcus and Bryce did.

"I found something!" Rob Roy called out, before he jumped backwards as several large boulders crashed from the ceiling to fill the space where only a heartbeat ago he had been standing.

"What was it? What did you find?" Marcus rushed forward as soon as the stones settled.

"'Twas a gap in the stone."

Marcus climbed on top of a boulder and peered through a small crack in the stone. "Rowena! Can you hear me?" Her name bounced off the stones and echoed back to him. Dust hung in the air as the earth stopped shaking. "Rowena!" Fear and horror and panic coiled in his stomach. Why didn't she answer?

A bleakness like nothing he'd ever known before tugged at his heart as a wash of memories tumbled through his mind. Rowena standing on the deck, looking out over the sea, or when she'd emerged from the waters of Dunvegan with seaweed in her hair, or when she stood next to him in the chapel, looking lovelier than he'd ever remembered when she pledged to love and honour him.

"Please," he pleaded as agony roiled his stomach. "Please let Rowena be alive."

"Marcus?" The word was faint, and at first he almost didn't believe he'd heard it until it came again. "Marcus."

He stared with one eye through the opening. "Rowena, are you there?"

Two fingers reached up and appeared at the edge of the rock. He reached his fingers inside and if he stretched he could just touch the tips of her fingers. "Oh, God, Rowena. How could I have failed you again?" She was behind all that rock, buried.

"It's not your fault, Marcus. I was the one who wandered off."

He pulled his hand back and started clawing at the rocks, trying to dislodge anything that would allow him to get to her, to save her.

"Marcus. I found the rest of the treasure. It's here in this tunnel."

"I don't give a damn about the treasure. I would give up every last piece if I could hold you in my arms once more."

He stopped scraping the boulders with his fingers and turned to Mack. "Go back to the ship and get any men who are willing to risk entering the cave. Bring black powder and a fuse as well as tools, anything that might help move these rocks. We only have a few hours before the tide turns again."

"Aye, Captain." Mack turned and raced out of the cave.

Marcus leaned his cheek against the cool, rugged stone, trying to draw a hint of Rowena's scent through the wall that separated them. The muffled sounds of crying reached through the rock and coiled around his heart.

"Don't cry," Marcus said in a ragged voice, reaching his hand back through the opening. "We are going to get you out."

"You and what miracle?" He could hear the sadness in her voice, feel her hopelessness.

It took a moment for her words to register, but when they did he straightened. *A miracle . . .*

"Hold on, Rowena. We are going to have you free in no time." Marcus pulled his fingers back. "Come, Rob Roy, Bryce. Help me try to dislodge this top rock."

The two men scrambled up to the top of the pile of boulders, and along with Marcus strained and tugged, trying with all their strength to move a rock that was no doubt heavier than the three of them together. After several long moments, they'd only managed to move it slightly. But they had moved it. "Let's keep trying," Marcus said, trying to fill his voice with enthusiasm.

Several minutes later, covered in sweat and exhausted by their efforts, they hadn't managed to move the boulder any farther. "Rob Roy, go and look for a sturdy branch or anything we might use to gain some leverage against this rock."

After Rob Roy ran off to do Marcus's bidding, he turned to Bryce. "I need you to stay here with Rowena."

"Where are you going?"

"There is something urgent I must do. I will return quickly. I promise." He would not fail again. He would not lose another man or woman in the pursuit of treasure. They'd tried moving the stones with brute force. Until they had an axe to smash the boulders into smaller chunks or a lever to shift them away from the gap, there wasn't much more in the physical sense he could do. But there was something of a more magical nature he had yet to try.

At Bryce's nod, Marcus raced back through the cave. When he reached the last piece of dry rock before it dipped into the sea, he paused, looking at the sky. In the cave he'd had no sense of the passing of time and was surprised to see the sun was already low on the horizon. If the morning's high tide had crested mid-morning, then the next high tide would happen around nine-thirty or ten o'clock that night. That meant they truly only had about four hours to free Rowena.

The paralysing fear that flashed through him at the thought had him sucking in a breath. He couldn't lose another person to the sea. Drawing another more steady breath, Marcus pushed the debilitating thought aside. He had a task to complete, there was no time for fear.

He stepped farther outside the cave, into the shallow water, and searched for a shell with two connecting halves. Nothing appeared on the dry land. Pressing his lips together, he searched the crystal-clear water at his feet, studying the rocks where molluscs could attach themselves. After serval moments he finally found what he was looking for. About five steps from the entrance of the cave was an empty mussel shell. Without hesitation, he waded more deeply into the water to retrieve the purple-blue shell.

Relying on folklore to help him at a time of need was not something he'd ever done before, but he would pray for divine intervention from a God who never seemed to answers his prayers; to Cliodna, the goddess of the sea; or any other deity who might help free Rowena from a terrible fate.

Marcus continued searching for a length of seaweed, to no avail. Only yellow-gold lichen grew around the edge of the cave. Frustrated, he moved back to dry land, and, hoping the goddess Cliodna would understand his predicament, he instead reached for the edge of his shirt and ripped off a thin length.

He closed his eyes, and holding the shell to his lips, whispered his wish into the two halves before closing it and tying it with the linen from his shirt. His gaze dropped to the water lapping at his feet. He watched, waiting for a larger surge than the others. As if in answer to his unspoken thoughts, a wave washed up over the top of his boots, bringing a momentary smile to his lips.

He counted each wave following until the ninth wave touched the rock. He had never asked for much in this life. Not in his own clan, not of the MacLeods, and perhaps not even of himself. The old Marcus was gone. A new one had been reborn in the darkness of the cave. From here on out, he would ask for love and warmth and joy from this world. And he intended to give back as much or more as he took.

Marcus straightened as a newfound strength seeped inside him. "I beg you, Cliodna, to answer my plea." He tossed the shell into the retreating wave. He waited as the roar of his voice echoed around him until there was only silence.

They only had three, perhaps four more hours to free Rowena. And release the woman he loved from the tunnel he would, even if he had to blast her out at the last moment and bring the rest of the cave down upon them. At least, using the powder meant he could hold her in his arms one last time as they drew their last breaths together.

ROWENA STOOD ROOTED in place at the realisation that the men on the other side of her could not move the boulders out of the way. Her knees went weak. Only sheer determination kept her from collapsing into a useless heap upon the cave's rock floor. Nay, it wasn't determination. It was grit, which she had in spades. All her life she'd had only herself to rely on.

For a golden moment in time, she'd had Marcus. She still did, but he was on the other side of the wall of rocks. If he could not move the boulders, it was up to her to find a way to free herself before she drowned. Her gaze dropped to the lantern in her hands and an idea occurred to her.

Once, when she'd been trapped between the walls of the castle in Dunvegan after the door Gwendolyn had told her about had closed on her and she'd lost her bearings, Rowena had found her way out of the maze using the flame from the brace of candles she'd taken with her. The flame had flickered when she'd discovered a source of air. Could she use the candle in the lantern to do the same thing? Could there possibly be another way into and out of the cave that didn't involve the passage now blocked by boulders?

She set the lantern down and bent to carefully withdraw the precious source of light. The candle flame was steady as she held it in her hands. Gathering her courage, she stood tall and moved back down to where she'd discovered the treasure. She hadn't noticed anything but the treasure the last time she was in that part of the cave. Hoping and praying there was something more, Rowena moved silently down the tunnel, her gaze trained on the flame.

Light slipped across the basalt walls and puddled on the

shadowy floor as she continued past the treasure. The only sounds in the cave were the click of her boots on the rock and her own breathing. Once she'd passed the point where Jacob Thorne had left his treasure, Rowena wondered if any other human had ever walked the path she did now.

The thought had barely materialised when Rowena stopped in the middle of the tunnel. Her gaze was fixed on the candle in her hands as the flame jumped before dancing towards the right. The flickering light meant there was a breeze coming from that direction. She turned and moved closer, casting the shadows away until she stood before yet another smaller opening in the rock near the floor.

A shiver ran down her spine at the sight of water lapping at the edges. Another opening, one with air, meant another way to possibly escape. The only way to know for certain was to dive in. But Rowena wasn't quite ready for that yet. There were multiple things to consider. Could she traverse the dark, water-filled tunnel and make it back to the surface of the sea before she could no longer hold her breath? Or did the air mean there were places where she could draw a breath before continuing? Were things so hopeless on the other end of the blocked tunnel that it was time to try something dangerous?

She set the candle down and lay down at the edge of the opening, trying to see into the blackness beyond the candle's illumination. If only she could have a sign that all might not end in disaster if she left the cave this way . . . Marcus might never recover if she died trying to swim her way to freedom.

Just then a dark object peeked out from the water's surface. A dark speckled head with two beady eyes stared straight at her. With a shriek, Rowena lurched back, scrambling to her feet, nearly knocking the candle over in the process. Her heart pounding in her ears, she grabbed the candle, desperate to maintain her source of light.

From a safer distance, she studied the head that had emerged from the water. She couldn't quite believe her eyes when she recognised it as a dark-skinned seal. Forcing her breathing into a normal pattern, she stepped closer and held out her hand to the sea creature. "How did you get in here?" If the seal had made it through whatever passageway lay ahead, could she also?

The seal floated towards her and pressed its nose against the tips of her fingers, then nudged her hand until it rested on its head. Not knowing what else to do, Rowena patted the creature lightly. "Are you trying to tell me something? That I can make it out of this cave with your help just like your kind helped me when I was in Loch Dunvegan?"

The seal barked, the sound echoing all around her. Hope flared inside her chest. Could she put her trust in the sea creature to guide her to safety in the darkness of the underwater tunnel? This was not a decision she could make alone, or at least make until she revealed to Marcus her true feelings.

Rowena looked into the animal's dark eyes, framed in

long lashes, and could see no malice, only a desire to help. Or was she reading the emotions she longed to see instead of what was truly there? With a deep sigh, Rowena patted the seal's head once more before drawing her hand back. "Will you wait for me while I go back to tell Marcus of this new plan?"

The seal barked. Would Marcus think she was mad to put her faith in the animals her mother feared? Rowena's gaze dropped to the candle in her hands. The wax had burned lower, perhaps even more than it should have since catching the flow of air in this portion of the cave.

With a final look at the seal, Rowena hurried back to Marcus. They had to decide what to do before it was too late.

CHAPTER NINETEEN

ECKLAND MACFARLANE STOOD at the railing of *The Cliodna* as the late afternoon sun was starting to head towards the horizon. He brought his spyglass up to see who was returning to the ship from the cave. He'd manoeuvred *The Cliodna* as close to the cave as he dared in order to make transferring the treasure as easy as possible. But the boat approaching him contained no treasure, and only one man, the boatswain known as Mack. The dark set of the young man's features told Eck that something was wrong.

Eck waited none too patiently for Mack to return to the ship and climb the ladder. The young man had barely put feet to deck when Eck greeted him. "What's wrong?"

"We found the captain and his wife after the water receded from the cave, but nae before tremors trapped the missus behind a wall of rock."

Eck's muscles tensed. "Is there any hope of dislodging the rocks?"

Grim-faced, Mack pursed his lips and a line formed between his brows. "It doesn't look good. I'd say we only have about four more hours tae mount a rescue before the offshoot of the cave she's in becomes flooded again."

At the arrival of one of their own, the other men aboard started to gather around.

"Damn his foul luck." Eck pushed his fingers through his hair as frustration coiled inside. "Why did the captain send you back here?"

"The captain wants powder and wicks, tools, and men, as many as are willing tae risk the possible dangers."

A cacophony of voices all raised at once, asserting their willingness to go help Marcus.

Eck raised two fingers to his mouth and released a loud whistle, instantly silencing the men. "I'll need ten men to stay back with me on this ship. The rest of you can gather the remaining boats and help your captain."

"I want tae go." Gordon strode forward to stand tall before Eck.

"You should be in the brig. How did you get out?" Eck frowned at the escaped prisoner.

"When I heard the captain's wife was trapped behind a wall of rock, I picked the lock and freed myself. I must go and help."

Eck glared down at the young man, exasperated. "That's not your choice to make."

"Before sailing on *The Cliodna* I was a stonemason. If any one of us knows anything about rocks, 'tis me." He lifted his shirt, exposing his back. "I'll take the lashes now in order to fulfil my punishment."

Eck pressed his lips together, thinking, then finally nodded. "All right. You can go, and there is no need for lashes either. If you can free Rowena, your sentence will be served."

"Thank you." Gordon lowered his shirt and stepped back amongst his crewmates to decide who would go with Gordon and Mack back to the cave. In the end, it was determined that they only had enough space on the boats for thirty men, ten in each. After tools were gathered and the powder and wicks placed in a small waterproof barrel, the men set off for *Uamh Oir*.

Eck stood at the rail and watched as the crew reached the cave, hoping and praying this time their treasure hunting would not end in tragedy.

"ROWENA? WHERE ARE you?" Marcus called through the slight opening in the rock. It was dark in the chamber where there had once been light. He'd returned to the blockage several minutes ago and Rowena had yet to answer him. Had she gone off exploring? He hoped that was all it was. Even so, as the moments of silence stretched out, he felt as though his heart was being cut from his chest. He forced himself to think through the pain, to ignore the incipient panic.

When finally he saw a light flare on the other side of the rocks, his heart soared. "Rowena?"

"I'm here, Marcus." She reached her fingers up to his,

touching the cold tips to his warmer ones.

"My men are here. So many of them from the ship came to help free you. Bryce is helping them bring supplies from the boats. It shouldn't be long now before you are free."

"Marcus." She drew a tremulous breath. "I found a way out as well."

"What do you mean?"

"There is a tunnel." She paused. "Except that it is below the water. I'm certain I can swim through it back out to the sea."

"Nay, Rowena. That sounds too risky."

"Riskier than trying to bring down these boulders in the next few hours?"

"If that fails then I'll send everyone away and blow the rocks with powder myself."

"And bring the entire cave down upon our heads. We'll both die, Marcus."

"We are running out of options." He tried and failed to keep the sound of defeat from his voice.

"Nay, we are not." Her fingers pushed farther into the opening so that he could feel more of her than before. "Something truly remarkable happened at the underwater tunnel. A seal came to the surface. The seals we saw earlier today know where I am and I think they want to help me escape."

"How can we trust seals with your life? Nay, Rowena, let my men at least try to free you."

She was silent for a long while before she finally said, "If that's what you want, then aye. Let's give your men two hours to see what they can do. But after that time has passed, I want to go back to the sea tunnel. I understand your fear. But, Marcus, back at Loch Dunvegan the darker-skinned seals helped me before. I honestly believe they will help me again. Perhaps it's because of the fairy armour, or because I'm a MacLeod, or because they know I truly need their assistance to survive. No matter the reason, I feel it deep inside my core that this is our only hope."

"You promised you'd give me and my men some time."

"I did. I will wait."

He released his breath in a rush. "I need you to climb down in order for them to start their work." He pulled his fingers from hers and scrambled down from his perch, giving his men full access to the solid pile of heavy rock.

TIME PASSED SLOWLY while Rowena leaned back against the wall of the cave. She watched the light in the lantern flicker as the wax burned lower. She would have blown out the candle but she had no way to light it again and the gap in the stone was too small to fit either a new candle or Marcus's flint and steel.

When, judging by the waning height of the candle, it had been over two hours and she had yet to see one boulder shift, she climbed back up to the small gap in the rocks. "Marcus?"

She could hear the grinding of stone and grunts from the men as they continued to battle the boulders. "Marcus," she tried again. This time the sounds stopped and she could hear someone climbing towards her.

"Rowena." Marcus's voice was laced with frustration.

"How are things progressing?"

"Slowly. We've managed to break up a few of the larger boulders towards the bottom only to find other boulders behind them. We need more time." His voice was suddenly quiet, almost strangled.

"Time is something none of us have. The candle is almost to its quick. If I am to make it back to the sea tunnel, I'll need a source of light." Rowena wet her suddenly trembling lips. "It's time, Marcus. I need to act now."

"Don't ask me to let you go, to lose you. Not when I finally know what I want." He shoved two fingers into the gap, searching for hers.

Instead of touching him, she pressed a kiss to the tips of his flesh, hoping and praying this would not be the end for them. "What is it that you want?"

"I want you. I thought you knew that." She heard the raw, aching need in his voice.

Her breath caught in her throat. "How would I know? I am not clairvoyant."

"I love you, Rowena, with all my heart. My actions must

have communicated how I felt about you."

"Sometimes a woman needs words."

He laughed, the sound a welcome relief to the pain and despair they'd both felt only moments ago. "Then in the future I pledge to not only show you with my actions but also to tell you with words how much I love you each and every day."

The future. A shower-burst of joy warmed all the places inside her that had become numb from the cold, wet cave. There were still many details that needed to be hashed out about their future, but that was for later. No matter the obstacles before them, they both had something to live for from this moment forward.

"It's going to be all right." She bent to kiss his fingertips once more. "I love you, Marcus. We will meet again in the water outside the cave." And with those words, she climbed down and picked up the lantern.

With a deep shuddering breath, she hurried down the tunnel. When she made it to where she'd found the treasure before she stopped, startled that the ten treasure chests were gone. With a frown, Rowena continued on to the sea tunnel, and setting the lantern down, knelt before the opening. The seal had also vanished. Her heartbeat thudded in her ears. She wasn't certain she could make her way through the pitch-black cave before her breath ran out without the seal's help.

Rowena waited several long moments, hoping the animal

would return. When it did not come, she gathered her courage and removed her boots, setting them next to the lantern. It would be easier to swim without her footwear weighing her down. Kneeling at the edge of the sea tunnel, Rowena vowed not to let this dark barrier rob her of the one thing she wanted most in this life—Marcus, and through him the resurrection of her dreams. She wouldn't drown in this tunnel and let everything they'd worked through over the past few days come to an end.

With a slow deep breath, she filled her lungs and dove head first into the ice-cold waters of the sea. The world took on a surreal quality. Time slowed. Only the sound of her own blood pulsing in her ears seemed real, as a cold darkness surrounded Rowena.

In the void it was difficult to tell up from down and right from left so she kicked her feet and pumped her arms, hoping and praying she was headed in the right direction. Instead of trying to fight the water, Rowena relaxed into it. That's when she felt it—a current that ebbed and flowed with the pulsing of the tide.

With a renewed sense of purpose and strength, Rowena followed the current. Twice she scraped her legs against something hard, most likely the side of the tunnel, but her fairy garments protected her from harm even as her chest burned. The need for air pressed in upon her as she continued on in the darkness.

Her lungs ached as she kicked her feet, ignoring the panic that edged into her thoughts. The tunnel was too deep, the surface too far away. Another realisation struck her as she kept moving forward. The cold water was sapping her strength. She hadn't counted on the water being so icy cold.

Pain ripped through Rowena's chest as the desire to draw breath took over rational thought. She pressed her lips tighter, fighting the instinct. When all of a sudden a dark object hurled towards her.

She almost gasped but stopped herself. Instead she flailed her arms in front of her, trying to swim past whatever blocked her way. Then her hands connected with something warm and solid. A fin perhaps? Holding on against hope that it was a seal, she tightened her grip and found herself jerked forward with a similar sensation of speed against the water that she'd felt in Loch Dunvegan.

Whatever she clung to propelled her towards air, life, and—she hoped—the future.

CHAPTER TWENTY

ARCUS HAD ORDERED everyone out of the cave as soon as the light had faded from the small gap in the blockade. If Rowena was going to swim out of the cave through some unknown channel, then he and his men would be waiting with their lanterns pushing back the darkness until they found her. They would wait all night if they had to for some sign that she had escaped.

Stars hung in the night sky, pinpoints of light that were the world's only illumination. The sea made an eternal blackness in all directions. Marcus closed his eyes. The stillness of the moment settled around him as he listened to the song of the wind stirring the sea, and waited for a splash that might indicate that Rowena had broken through to the surface.

Please, Cliodna, help Rowena survive. He sent his silent plea heavenward as they waited.

He'd asked that all the lanterns except one per boat be extinguished while all five of the boats left the cave and had positioned themselves across the area around it. He'd wanted to save the candlelight for when they needed it.

When the sound of something large breaking through the surface of the water came to him, Marcus called out, "Light the lanterns."

One by one the lights on the boats overtook the stars overhead, turning back the night and casting a golden glow across the surface of the sea. "Rowena!" Marcus called out, searching for any indication that she had arrived safely.

Only the sound of the waves lapping against the rocky shoreline came to him, until on his left a seal barked once, then twice. "Row towards the seals," Marcus ordered as he searched the water for Rowena. The dark leather of her clothing and dark hair made spotting her in the hazy light that much more difficult.

The splashing of water and the barking of the seals continued until Marcus finally saw not only the sea animals, but also a still form between them. They were nosing and bumping Rowena, her head bobbing mostly out of the water with the waves they created by playing with her form. As the boat drew near, Marcus reached over the side and, grasping Rowena by her arms, dragged her into the boat. He settled her body on the bottom of the boat. She did not respond. She did not move as she lay against the wood, pale and lifeless. "Nay!" His heart clogged his throat. "Please, don't take her from me now."

Time stopped as Marcus rolled her on her side and pounded, again and again, on her back. "Don't . . . leave . . . me," he cried as an emptiness crept inside his soul. "I love you."

Marcus froze as he heard a slight intake of breath. The sound was faint, but it made his heart soar. He waited as Rowena coughed up water. When she was through, he pulled her into his arms and watched her eyes open. "You made it out."

"Not alone." Her voice was rough. "I never would have survived if the seals hadn't helped me."

Marcus pulled her tighter against his chest and looked out over the water as the lantern light dotted the landscape. It was a beautiful sight. Silently he thanked Cliodna for this miracle and he nodded his appreciation to the seals who disappeared a moment later.

"The treasure." Rowena drew a ragged breath.

"Hush," Marcus soothed. "None of us here care about the treasure any longer. Only that you made it out alive."

The six crewmen in the boat nodded their agreement. "Those of us who came on this journey will all return home alive," said Bryce. "Nothing means more than that."

"Tell the others to head back to the ship," Marcus ordered Bryce, returning his attention to the woman in his arms. She was safe. She was where she belonged. He buried his face in her hair and breathed in the scent of her that the salt water had not been able to wash away—that elusive, unforgettable scent of sunshine and heather.

She hugged him and for a moment they remained wrapped in each other as everything that had stood between them before faded away. They were both committed to making a future together. They would find some way to honour his lost men while remaining together.

———✦———

BACK ON THE ship, the crew greeted Marcus with cheers, and welcomed Rowena back with exclamations of relief. The cook had brought a barrel of ale up on deck for the men to drink as they celebrated their successful rescue. At the joy surrounding her, Rowena's chest felt unaccountably tight. These men no longer saw her as a visitor but as one of the crew. And they did not blame her for their lost fortune.

"Come," Marcus said holding out his hand to her. "Let's get you out of those wet clothes."

Instead of taking Marcus's hand, she removed the leather pouch, containing the pearls from her tunic. "This is all that remains of the ten other treasure chests in the cave. It should be distributed to the crew just as the remainder of the treasure will be."

He took the pouch. "Do you mean to say the rest of the treasure is gone?"

She nodded. "It vanished after I happened upon it the first time."

After a collective gasp, the crewmen surrounding them started to talk amongst themselves.

"The treasure has vanished?" Rob Roy asked.

Mack's eyes widened. "'Twas taken by the selkie fowk. I saw the beings in the water when we rescued the missus."

"Selkies are nae real," Gordon said with his hands on his hips. "None of the myths surrounding *Uamh Oir* were real. There was no dog, no entrance to Fairyland or Hell, and we all came out alive."

"For that miracle we can be grateful," Marcus replied, offering Rowena his hand once more. She accepted it and they headed for the captain's quarters. Behind them the men continued to theorise about the treasure's whereabouts. Rowena blocked out the sound. Her thoughts were no longer on the treasure, but on the man at her side.

Before she and Marcus reached the cabin, Bryce stopped them. "I want to let you both know that I no longer want to keep the gold we found in the cave all to myself. I want to share it amongst the crew. And—" he dropped his gaze to his feet "—I want to apologise to you, Rowena, for threatening to harm you. I now know how wrong that was."

Bryce brought his gaze to Marcus. "Since I was a child I idolised you, Marcus. Remember how I used to follow you around, trying to imitate all that you did? You were so much better at everything than I was." He sighed. "Instead of trying harder, jealousy took hold. Over the years, that resentment only intensified as the clan pushed me further away because of my lack of skill and commitment. I see now that instead of coveting the things you had, I should have continued to try to be more like you. I've caused you both great harm in the past year and I truly regret all that I've done."

"You could be so much more than you are allowing yourself, Bryce. Surround yourself with good people, listen and learn from them and you'll be a different man." Marcus clapped his cousin on the shoulder.

Rowena released Marcus's hand and stepped closer to Bryce. "I forgive you for everything. From the first moment we met, I could sense your desperation and your lack of purpose. I hope our adventure has helped you find a part of yourself that you might have never known existed."

His gaze connected with hers—a gaze filled with remorse as well as a newfound pride. "It has." He turned back to Marcus. "Cousin, I know I have no right to ask you this . . . Will you teach me to sail? I have felt more at home on this ship over the last few days than I ever felt in the midst of our clan."

Marcus nodded. "Aye, Bryce. I will teach you to sail. In fact, I will teach you how to run an entire ship."

The smile that came to Bryce's lips transformed his features. Instead of his usual dark, angry countenance, hope and joy shone from his dark eyes. "Thank you, both of you. I'll leave you in peace now that I've had my say. And thank you for not giving up on me. You are the only two people in my life who never did." He turned away. Then over his shoulder said, "See you both in the morning."

Rowena stared after Bryce until he disappeared below

deck before turning back to Marcus. "Only a few days ago I would have thought such a change in Bryce was impossible."

"It appears this voyage has changed many a heart, including mine." He studied her eyes as he gently framed her face with his hands. "Welcome to the start of our new life together, Mrs MacDonald."

Tears of happiness welled in her eyes at the idea that Marcus had fully accepted her as his wife. She'd almost given up ever feeling such joy again once they'd left Dunvegan. That same emotion tightened her chest and filled her heart to overflowing. She raised her hands and covered his with them. "Shall we retire for the night, Mr MacDonald?"

He led her inside the captain's quarters and closed the door before leaning closer and kissing her, gently, slowly, as if they had all the time in the world. There in the soft candlelight, they celebrated all they had now, all they'd reclaimed. All the passion, life, and gifts love had to offer. They showed their love for each other with their hands, their lips, their mouths, until that emotion radiated through every part of their souls.

In harmony, they crested the peak of ecstasy, gasping, clinging to each other, celebrating the beginning of their new life together and the fact that they were still both alive after their adventures in *Uamh Oir*.

They had found treasure in the cave, just not the one they had expected. In their desperation, they'd laid their souls bare and had released their own individual goals into the darkness, allowing them to try to build new goals and dreams together.

Throughout the night love drove them, racked them, enfolded them in its grace. And when morning came, they knew they'd found a new dream for the rest of their lives.

Rowena stirred as morning light streamed through the windows, bathing the man who held her tight against his chest in hues of gold and bronze. It seemed the sun had come out to send them on their journey home. Not wanting to end the bliss of last night, Rowena held the moment and Marcus close, wrapping herself in their joined warmth with a smile on her face.

"What are you smiling about, Wife?"

She felt him shift in the bed so that he was lying back against the pillows, gazing down at her. "I am taking in the moment because once we leave this bed, decisions must be made. That might set us at odds again. I'm not ready for that."

"What decisions would those be?"

The moment had come long before she wanted it to. She sat up and faced her husband. "I will not let you abandon me at Dunvegan for a year while you make amends to the families of those you lost. I have an idea . . ." A sharp rap on the cabin's door interrupted the moment.

Marcus moved from the bed and stepped into his breeches while she reached for her shift. The fairy garments she'd worn last night were still damp. Until they dried she'd have to wear one of her gowns.

A second hurried knock sounded before Marcus pulled his shirt over his head. "Captain. The men have something they wish to discuss with you." Eck's voice sounded on the opposite side of the door.

Marcus pulled the door open once Rowena had fastened her gown. "What's wrong?"

Eck's eyes widened when he took in Marcus's dishevelled state. "My apologies, I assumed you'd be up by now. Nothing is wrong. The men simply want to have a word with their captain and his lovely wife." Eck's gaze strayed to where Rowena sat buckling her slippers. She would have to replace her boots as soon as possible, for delicate slippers had no real value on a ship. When she was through, she came to join Marcus at the door.

A pleased smile touched Marcus's lips as he slipped his arm about her. "I was in no hurry to leave this cabin after all Rowena and I have endured. I had expected you to handle our departure."

"You are both strong and have wills of iron. It takes a great deal to rend iron." A tender smile lit Eck's face. "Rowena, since coming aboard this ship you have already performed one miracle by healing Marcus's grief. Together you will heal from your time in the cave, and then you will continue to thrive in each other's company, I have no doubt." Eck straightened and the softness left his features. "But enough about how lucky the two of you are to have each other. As I said, the men wish an audience."

"Give us a moment to pull ourselves together," Marcus said.

Eck nodded. "The men are gathered on the main deck."

"Everyone?" Marcus asked with a hint of surprise in his voice.

"Every last man." Eck turned and left them to finish dressing.

When Marcus and Rowena stepped from the cabin a few moments later all the men were lined up in rows of eight, seven deep. Mack, Rob Roy, Gordon, and Bryce stood at the front of those assembled. With her arm resting on his, Marcus led Rowena up two steps of the quarterdeck so they could see the entire crew.

Bryce stepped forward at the edge of the bottom step. "You've expressed your desire to make settlements on the families of the men who died while trying to retrieve the treasure of Sandwood Bay. That task could take you away from not only your wife, but also the men who currently serve you aboard *The Cliodna*.

"The men and I gathered last night and came up with a proposal we'd like to offer you that would accomplish the task of disbursement much more quickly."

Marcus arched a brow. "I'm listening."

"What would you think if we broke ourselves into four teams that would head to north, south, east, and west of Scotland and the Isles, seeking these families. One team would be led by you, one by me, one by Eck, and one by Gordon. We could carry out the task in a matter of months."

"Who would stay with the ship?"

Bryce smiled. "Why, you and Rowena of course. You would sail to the western locations, then deliver a portion of the treasure to each family by horse. While you are gone from the ship, Mack will oversee the anchored vessel."

Marcus pressed his lips together, considering. "How do you propose to keep the portion of treasure you carry safe while traveling, especially through areas where there are known English patrols?"

"We rely on our clans. The twelve men I lead will first head to clan MacDonald and gather a small army of men to accompany us. I know that even I can find twelve MacDonalds to help if I pay them a few gold coins from the treasure we recovered from the Cave of Gold."

"I will travel to the MacPherson clan to gather men," Gordon said, stepping forward to join Bryce.

"The MacFarlanes will aid me, of that I have no doubt," Eck said from his position beside the men.

Marcus's brows furrowed. "You would all do that? Give up two months of your life to help reconcile the debts owed to our fallen brothers?"

"Aye, Captain," the crew said in unison, the sound echoing through the morning stillness.

Rob Roy smiled. "You've made us all rich men, Captain. It's the least we can do."

Rowena swung to face her husband. "Before we were interrupted this morning by Eck, I was going to suggest that I go with you, wearing my fairy armour and disguised as one of your men."

Marcus reached up to gently smooth a lock of her dark hair from her temple. "No one could ever mistake you for a male, my love, but I accept your offer." He turned back to his men. "Given the amount of thought and heart you put into this plan, I have nothing to say but aye and thank you."

Cheers rose up from the men. When silence settled over them once more, Marcus smiled a little sadly as his gaze passed over those assembled. "Then it appears we will have one last voyage back to Dunvegan together. We can leave your allotments of the treasure there for you to retrieve when the task of honouring our fallen crewmen is done. Then I will have the burden of finding worthy men such as yourselves to replace you."

"My brither will sail with ye," a tall, dark-haired sailor called from the back of those gathered.

"As would my cousin," Fergus said.

"I've two cousins that would relish the chance tae learn tae sail," said Naill. Others echoed that sentiment.

"Sounds as if I will have a full complement of fine replacements." Marcus's gaze was a warm caress, embracing them all as the men went back to their posts, preparing for their departure.

Rowena suddenly realised that the men were more than

crewmen. They were Marcus's family. "These men love and respect you very much."

A sudden warm smile lit Marcus's face. "I love them too. That was why losing so many of them was so hard on me." Marcus's arms came around Rowena from behind and he drew her back against him. His lips gently brushed her temple. "Eck was right. You helped heal the pain of loss and gave me something to hold on to for our future together."

Rowena turned in his arms, facing him. "I've given you nothing."

"You've given me everything, my love. When I had no clan you took me in. When I had no home, you wrapped me in your arms. When I had no family, you gave me something to hope for in the birth of our first child." His hand moved down to cover her abdomen.

"We cannot know for certain."

"I know. And so do you."

She did know. Their first night together had given them a child that would bind them in a way even their marriage vows could not. The effects on her body were already evident. She was softer in some places and fuller in others.

"In all the commotion of last night I forgot to ask you . . . You mentioned the remaining ten treasure chests were missing from the cave when you went back to the sea tunnel. I find that odd."

"The only explanation for their disappearance is that the seals took them."

He frowned. "What would seals want with treasure?"

She shrugged. "Perhaps it is like a raven with a shiny object. The seals don't think of the goods as treasure, only something interesting to play with. Unless of course they are not seals at all but the selkie fowk."

"We may never know."

"You're not upset about losing the riches?"

Marcus leaned forward and placed a kiss on her lips. "The only treasure I ever need is right here in my arms. Besides, I did not make a good privateer. All the treasure I plundered was given to me by Jacob Thorne."

"Not given," Rowena corrected. "You had the arduous task of recovering it from the bottom of the sea and deep inside the Cave of Gold."

"True, but all that was still easier than finding treasure myself."

"Did you ever think that you were given the gift of the treasure for a reason? When you started this journey eight months ago, you left alone with a hired crew you knew nothing about. Now Eck is a dear friend, and your men have proven they will do anything for you."

"They are good men. A rare thing these days." With a smile he gathered her against his chest. "Good women even more unusual."

"And now you have an extraordinary, fearless woman as your partner for life." She wrapped her arms around his neck as laughter spilled from him.

"Extraordinary, indeed!"

After a long kiss, Rowena stepped back. "Now that we know how we can stay together in the weeks ahead, I have a treasure to finish counting and you need to take us home to Dunvegan so we can tell my brothers of our future plans."

Marcus's face was still wreathed in a smile as he stepped back, clicked his boot heels together, and offered her a salute. "By your command, my Highland bride."

CHAPTER TWENTY-ONE

THEY ARRIVED BACK at Dunvegan two days later. The castle was a flurry of activity, but they had no idea why until they found Mrs Morgan pacing at the top of the stairwell. When the chatelaine saw Rowena her eyes rounded. "Oh, thank goodness, yer home. Gwendolyn's in labour."

Rowena hurried up the stairs, leaving Marcus behind. "Are Gwendolyn and the baby all right? Is Lottie with her?" The short woman's face was filled with a tension that brought a sudden tightness to Rowena's chest.

"Lottie, Alastair, and Fiona are in the laird's bedchamber with her, but it's been so long since we've had a babe in this castle I'm nae certain what I should do? Boil water? Bring clean linens? Go tae the chapel and pray?"

"Prayers never hurt," Rowena said, feeling some of her own tension ease. Mrs Morgan had cared for them all for so long. Over the years, she'd bandaged their scraped knees, and had listened when they needed someone to talk to. But easing Gwendolyn's pain during childbirth was not something she could fix so easily. "Why don't you go to the chapel and say a prayer or two until you feel more at ease. I'll go see if Lottie needs anything. Would that be all right with you?"

The ageing redhead nodded. "So good of you to arrive when you did. Gwendolyn needs you."

Rowena took two steps and stopped, glancing back at Marcus. "This was not how we planned our return."

"If we've learned anything in the past few days it is to expect the unexpected. You go ahead. I will see Mrs Morgan to the chapel before going to find Tormod."

Rowena hurried down the long hallway to the laird's chamber. She knocked on the door and was greeted by Fiona who instantly wrapped her in a ferocious hug.

"You've returned!"

"Just in time, I see, to welcome the new babe into our clan." The birth of a child was always a beautiful thing, but there were dangers as well. "How is Gwendolyn doing? Isn't she in her eighth month? The baby is early. Will it survive?"

Fiona stepped aside. "Come and see how mother and child fare for yourself."

As Rowena entered the chamber, she was struck by the sight of Alastair sitting near the bed. He brought a cool cloth up to bathe Gwendolyn's temple, brushing away with each new contraction the sweat that gathered on her brow. Tears came to Rowena's eyes. "He really does love her, doesn't he?"

"Aye." Fiona's gaze shifted from Gwendolyn back to Rowena. Fiona's eyes narrowed for a moment then the faintest smile tugged at her lips. "It seems all of us have been blessed when it comes to matters of the heart." She brought a hand to rest upon her own and then Rowena's abdomen. "We are both with child," she whispered.

"Congratulations, Fiona. I'm so pleased for you and Tormod," she whispered back to her sister-in-law as she shook her head dazedly. "How could you know that I am . . .? It hasn't been long enough to be certain."

"I have been watching Gwendolyn for the last eight months, and my own image in the looking glass for the last two."

"You could have told me."

Fiona smiled. "It was Gwendolyn's time. Our secrets can wait for a while longer."

Gwendolyn cried out as another contraction overtook her body. Alastair drew his wife's hand to his lips and pressed a kiss at the centre.

"Come help me with the linens," Fiona said, letting their secret bind them as they moved to help their sister bring new life into the world.

MARCUS FOUND TORMOD and Graeme outside of the castle, walking backwards in the courtyard. They stopped walking when they saw him and waved him over.

"The privateer has returned," Tormod greeted with a

welcoming smile. "Were you successful in your treasure hunting?"

"We recovered four chests of gold."

"That is significant." Graeme raised his brows. "What will you do with all that bounty? Or has Bryce already taken it for his own?"

"Bryce, it seems, simply needed a few hard lessons about life to alter his thinking. He's changed since we left Dunvegan a week ago."

Both men shared a glance, just as Aria appeared in the doorway of the castle with her hands on her hips, setting Tormod and Graeme in motion around the courtyard again. "Come, join us." Tormod gestured for Marcus to fall in step with them.

"Why are you doing this?" Marcus asked, falling into step with the other men.

"Lottie says the men of the castle walking backwards during Gwendolyn's labour will ease her pains," Graeme replied.

Tormod chuckled. "I am certain 'tis simply a way for the womenfolk to keep the men out of the way while the baby is born."

Marcus's lips pulled up in a grin. "Where's Alastair?"

"He refused to leave Gwendolyn's side." Tormod clapped Marcus on the shoulder. "So tell us, Brother, how fares our sister? Is she changed as well?" Tormod's amusement was suddenly replaced with a seriousness.

Marcus averted his gaze. Should he tell them the truth?

He didn't want any secrets between him and his new family no matter how they might react. Marcus stopped walking. "She is well now, but we had a few difficulties while trying to recover the treasure from the Cave of Gold."

Tormod froze. A deep frown darkened his features. "Explain yourself."

Marcus recounted all their troubles, from the saboteur aboard the ship to the tide trapping them and the earthquake trapping Rowena. When he had finished with his tale, both men stared at him with befuddled expressions on their faces. "The seals helped Rowena make it through the tunnel?"

"Rowena believes they were the same seals who inhabit the small isles near Dunvegan. Several appeared to follow us on our journey."

"Seals or selkie fowk?" Graeme's expression became thoughtful.

Marcus shrugged. "It matters not to me. Only that Rowena is safe."

"Now that you've returned to dry land, let us hope that is the last time Rowena will have any connection to the fairy realm." Tormod drew a deep breath and released it. "This clan has had more encounters with fairies and otherworldly fowk than any members of our clan before Ian Cair, our ancestor who brought us the Fairy Flag."

Graeme's gaze drifted to the path leading to the fairy bridge. "This clan's interactions with the fairies are far from over, Tormod. Alastair intends to go in search of your missing brother."

Tormod grimaced. "Back to Fairyland? Is that even possible?"

Graeme's jaw firmed. "Aria came to us from such a place. Perhaps she can help us return and bring Keiran home after all these years. Then we will all be together once more as a family. Perhaps that is the last piece of helping your mother finally move from this plane of existence and into the great beyond."

"Not all of us will be together," Marcus interjected. "Rowena and I are not done with the sea just yet. For I still must settle a portion of the treasure on each of the families of the men I've lost during our treasure hunting."

"Rowena was to remain here while you accomplished that task." Tormod's spine was suddenly stiff. "The sea is a dangerous place for a woman, as you've already explained from your earlier troubles."

Marcus shook his head. "I cannot be parted from her for a moment longer than necessary. Besides, your sister is stronger than any of you realise."

Tormod suddenly smiled. "I believe the MacLeod women are more resilient and tougher than any of us men."

As if proving his point, the healthy cry of a baby resounded, making its way to them through the open castle doors. "The baby is here." A few moments later the sound of another cry came to the men.

A moment later Aria appeared, framed by the doorway

and wreathed in a smile. "Gwendolyn has given birth to not one, but two sons."

THE ENTIRE HOUSEHOLD gathered along the shores of Loch Dunvegan to send Rowena and Marcus on their way, along with twelve MacLeod warriors selected by Tormod to help them safely deliver treasure to the families that she and Marcus would visit over the next several weeks.

Pain knifed through Rowena when memories swelled as she took in the golden-brown stones of Dunvegan in the distance. Reuniting with Gwendolyn after five long years, Fiona and the fairy armour, her brothers' protectiveness, Aria fighting alongside the other women of the clan, her mother's ghostly appearance that grew more fully human as each of her children found happiness, Mrs Morgan's unconditional love, Mrs Honey's tasty treats, being held prisoner by the MacDonalds, but being freed by Marcus's parents, Bryce kidnapping her, yet now he was a part of their family too. The MacDonalds and the MacLeods had a new reason to set aside their disputes because of the child she now carried that belonged to both clans.

It might be optimistic to hope her and Marcus's child could bring an end to warring between the two clans. Her hand strayed to her abdomen, covering the new life that fluttered there. Rowena would never give up on that possibility. She'd seen too many miracles happen in her family as of late not to believe in one that would change all their lives forever.

Peace.

Marcus turned to her and concern lit his face. "What is it? What's wrong?"

Rowena smiled. "Nothing is wrong. I was simply thinking back on all the memories here in this place."

"We are not leaving forever." Marcus took her hand in his. "When we do finally settle back on land, we'll find somewhere close to your family to build our own memories. We are starting a new life together, my love."

"Aye, we are, and those we leave behind will flourish in our absence."

Alastair and Gwendolyn came forward, each with a swaddled babe in the lee of their arms. A look of exquisite tenderness came over Alastair's face as he looked at his two sons. The babes were so small. So beautiful.

"Do you have names for your children yet?" Rowena asked, reaching out to touch the tiny hand of the child in her brother's arms.

"This little rascal is Rory." Alastair turned to Gwendolyn. The child in her arms nestled against her body, seeking warmth and comfort from its mother. "This is Jarlath." A look of utter satisfaction rode Alastair's features as he brought his gaze back to her and Marcus. "Come back to us soon. Our family is not complete without the two of you."

"Always," Rowena said as she stepped forward and pressed a kiss to her brother's cheek and wrapped Gwendolyn in a warm embrace. Unshed tears burned Rowena's throat as she and Marcus headed to the boat that would take them back to *The Cliodna*.

"Does leaving your family make you sad?" Marcus asked as they rowed away from shore.

"Nay." She hesitated. "Aye. I don't know for certain. My feelings vacillate from moment to moment. My family is all I've ever known." She pulled her gaze from the shore to look at her husband. "One thing is for certain. I want to be with you, wherever you are, on the sea or on land. The rest of it will fall into place as it should."

"I couldn't agree with you more." Marcus pulled her close and in silence they watched as the coastline of Dunvegan Castle faded into the distance.

CHAPTER TWENTY-TWO

Back aboard *THE Cliodna*, Rowena stepped from the captain's quarters and stood in the sunlight shining down from overhead. Bathed in golden rays, Marcus thought she looked like the goddess Cliodna herself, while her full skirt was caught by the wind to billow around her legs as she came closer. Rowena's glorious hair had been swept up and piled high, tendrils allowed to trail down either side of her face.

"You're beautiful," Marcus said in a low rasping whisper when she reached him.

Rowena laughed. Her cheeks bloomed with colour as she looked around the upper decks of the ship. "Where is everyone?"

The two of them were very much alone. "The crew are all below deck except Eck, who is keeping a low profile as he mans the till. We are in deep water and the wind is fair. Fear not. All is well for a short while."

Marcus smiled at her as he opened his folded hands to reveal the emerald necklace he had once given to her. "You said you would have nowhere to wear this, so I wanted to give you the opportunity here with me, tonight. Will you wear this necklace for me, Rowena?"

She nodded.

He reached up and fastened the necklace about her neck, allowing his hand to follow the emeralds down to the centre stone. "Tonight, you are the goddess Cliodna and the queen of my heart." He bowed to her and extended his hand. "May I have this dance?"

"There's no music," Rowena said even as she walked into his arms.

"Ah, but there is. Listen to the whisper of the wind upon the sails, the thrumming of the rigging, and the crescendo of the waves as they break against the bow of the ship. It's the music of the sea, my love, created just for you tonight." Marcus slid his right arm around her waist, bringing her close against the solid wall of his body. His left hand closed around her fingers, engulfing them as he gently whirled her around the deck.

He gazed down into her glorious hazel eyes, and he tightened his arms, pulling her even closer, until his lips brushed her hair. Since their time together in the Cave of Gold, Marcus had felt more at ease, no longer burdened by guilt, and more hopeful than he ever imagined about the future.

"Will you accept my gift of these emeralds, Rowena, and wear them for me on special occasions that might occur in our future together?"

She pressed her lips together considering, yet a smile

tugged at her lips. "Nay. I don't think I will."

He raised a brow. "Then when will you wear them?"

"I wish to wear them on Saturdays, and on picnics in the moors, and anytime we walk along the shores of Scotland."

Marcus smiled down at his wife. When her steps slowed, he followed. "What changed your mind?"

"Something as beautiful as these emeralds should not be hidden away in a jewellery case. Besides, I don't want you to look at these stones and remember what you lost. Instead, I want you to look upon them and only think of the goodness in our lives." Her eyes were brilliant and filled with hope. "The truest treasure of life is not silver, gold, and gemstones, but love."

Hope for their future filled his heart as he stopped dancing and pulled back to gaze upon her flat abdomen. Very soon they would have signs of new life to look forward to. He reached up and brushed a lock of her hair away from her cheek, relishing the rich, silky feel and the knowledge that he had the rest of his life to touch her. "You are the true treasure of my life, Rowena. Where family begins, love never ends."

THE END

Want more? Check out Orrick and Isolde's story in
To Win a Highlander's Heart!

Join Tule Publishing's newsletter for more great reads and weekly deals!

Author's Note

The Isle of Skye is a truly magical place. Within its shores can be found escarpments and needle-like pinnacles. Mist-shrouded mountains tower over heather-clad glens, shimmering lochs, and wild moors.

The coastline features stacks, arches, caves, sweeping bays, and great sea cliffs. Waterfalls plunge into steely blue seas, and powerful tidal streams surge around the sea lochs, menacing the unwary.

The Cave of Gold or *Uamh Oir* is one of those coastal treasures located five miles north of Uig, Scotland. The cave is one of the most secluded and unknown spots on the Isle of Skye. Despite the many legends of gold deep within the cave's depths, the Cave of Gold's name is most likely derived from the yellow lichen that cover the basalt rock formations near its entrance.

The mythology surrounding the cave is varied, as each generation creates new ways to keep unwanted visitors from exploring the dark and dangerous depths.

Celtic lore abounds in Scotland. One such tale is that of the goddess Cliodna, pronounced KLEE-nah. She is the Celtic goddess of love who presided over the Celtic Otherworld. In Celtic mythology, the Otherworld is a great realm of all deities and also the realm of the dead. It is often described as a supernatural world of youth, beauty, joy, and abundance. Cliodna was said to be quite beautiful, but despite her beauty she had a darker side.

One tale claims Cliodna used her beauty to lure mortals to their deaths by the shoreline, and thus creating the superstition that it was bad luck for a sailor to see a woman before travelling off to sea. Another tale tells of how she fell in love with a mortal, deciding to become mortal herself, then drowned in the harbour of Glandore. As a constant reminder of her presence, every ninth wave that crashes against the shore is known as Cliodna's wave.

All treasure-hunting books need a lost treasure to find. *To Claim His Highland Bride* is no different. The Cave of Gold seemed a perfect location to hide a lost treasure. The treasure hidden inside was that of *The Santisima Concepcion*, also known as *El Grande. El Grande* was a massive Spanish galleon commanded by Admiral Manual Ortiz Aosemena when it sank in sixteen hundred and eighty-three. *El Grande* was carrying a treasure bound for Spain, when it ran into the hurricane that sank it and killed four hundred and ninety-six men on board. Only four men made it to the shores of Saint Augustine, Florida, but the ship and its treasure was never found.

El Grande was said to be carrying silver bullion, spices, fifteen hundred pounds of gold, seventy-seven chests of pearls, two hundred seventeen chests of other goods, and forty-nine chests of emeralds.

Legend has it that only a single chest filled with clothes and fifteen hundred pesos ever washed ashore in Florida. It was believed to belong to the wreck. Recovery efforts went on until around seventeen hundred and one, but *El Grande* has never been found. It may be somewhere in the waters of Key Biscayne or anywhere between the Florida coast and the Bahamas . . . or farther out in the Atlantic Ocean where a fictional treasure hunter named Jacob Thorne might have discovered just a portion of the bounty that had once been on board that mighty ship.

If you enjoyed *To Claim His Highland Bride*,
you'll love the other books in the...

GUARDIANS OF THE ISLES SERIES

Book 1: *The Return of the Heir*

Book 2: *Only a Highlander Will Do*

Book 3: *To Win a Highlander's Heart*

Book 4: *To Claim His Highland Bride*

Available now at your favorite online retailer!

More books by Gerri Russell

All the Kings Men series

Book 1: *Seven Nights with a Scot*

Book 2: *Romancing the Laird*

Book 3: *A Temptress in Tartan*

Book 4: *A Laird and a Gentleman*

Book 5: *Much Ado About a Scot*

Available now at your favorite online retailer!

ABOUT THE AUTHOR

Barbara Roser Photography

Gerri Russell is the award-winning author of historical and contemporary novels including the Brotherhood of the Scottish Templars series and *Flirting with Felicity*. A two-time recipient of the Romance Writers of America's Golden Heart Award and winner of the American Title II competition sponsored by *RT Book Reviews* magazine, she is best known for her adventurous and emotionally intense novels set in the thirteenth- and fourteenth-century Scottish Highlands. Before Gerri followed her passion for writing romance novels, she worked as a broadcast journalist, a newspaper reporter, a magazine columnist, a technical writer and editor, and an instructional designer. She lives in the Pacific Northwest with her husband and four mischievous black cats.

Thank you for reading

To Claim His Highland Bride

If you enjoyed this book, you can find more from all our great authors at TulePublishing.com, or from your favorite online retailer.

TULE

Made in the USA
Coppell, TX
07 February 2025

45520176R10163